STARSTRUCK

STARSTRUCK

Suzanne Goodwin

This title first published in Great Britain 1997 by
SEVERN HOUSE PUBLISHERS LTD of
9–15 High Street, Sutton, Surrey SM1 1DF.
Originally published in 1969 in Great Britain as A
Most Auspicious Star and pseudonym of *Suzanne Ebel*.
This title first published in the U.S.A. 1998 by
SEVERN HOUSE PUBLISHERS INC of
595 Madison Avenue, New York, N.Y. 10022.

British Library Cataloguing in Publication Data

Goodwin, Suzanne

   Starstruck
   1.   Love stories
   I.   Title
   823.9'14 [F]

   ISBN 0 7278 5274 4

Typeset by Palimpsest Book Production Limited,
Polmont, Stirlingshire, Scotland.
Printed and bound in Great Britain by
MPG Books Ltd, Bodmin, Cornwall.

I find my zenith doth depend upon
A most auspicious star."
Prospero in **The Tempest**

I

The trouble with being an actress is that you think of nothing else. Tamara Waring walked down the passage towards the study of her father's house; it was a crisp autumn day, the windows were open and the michaelmas daisies in the garden were five foot high; the lawn was strewn with leaves the colour of lemons. But Tamara didn't spare them a look. She went straight to the study door.

"Am I allowed in?"

The man at the desk laughed.

"Don't be ridiculous."

She didn't budge.

"When I called yesterday, Dad threw me straight out again."

"You know when it's like that there's nothing I can do to help. Do come *in*!" said Bernard.

Satisfied by the tone, she strolled into the room, getting an undisguised look of admiration even though, feature by feature, she was not beautiful. Her face was too round for an actress, her nose was snub, and if she didn't slim most of the time she would certainly have had a small double chin. She had a habit of anxiously examining her profile in the mirror, grasping her throat in one hand, as one might grasp the jowl of a puppy. She was five foot two, and on stage it is an advantage to be tall. But Tam was the daughter of a star and had inherited from him a kind of extra dimension. She made you stare.

She walked over to Bernard's desk and sat herself on top of it, squashing some manuscripts and just missing a bottle of ink. Leaning over so that he could smell the scent she'd sprayed over her neck, she took some pencils from a jar.

7

She began to push them, one after the other at different angles, into her hair.

"Just tell me what advantage there is in having a famous father when one gets ordered into the garden for asking him a few questions about one's job?" she said, giving Bernard a slow-burn smile.

He looked pleased.

Bernard was nearing thirty, burly, with cropped black hair, small ears, and the look of a sportsman running to fat. He had broad shoulders and a nature to match. Sir Robert Waring, Tamara's father, approved of Bernard's solidity. "That chap who owns the Steel Corporation told me he prefers men with ulcers," he'd said to Tamara when they discussed Bernard. "There are quite enough ulcers in the theatre; how I detest stomach powder in the dressing-rooms! I like someone who plays the straight man : the healthy heavy."

Tam was now fond of Bernard, and saw her father's point about the "healthy heavy," whom she used to help her.

Her hair bristling with red and yellow pencils, she turned a look on Bernard which said : "Admire me."

"Don't you think I'd make a good Geisha," she said. "We could have the tea ceremony. Sit on the floor facing each other, and I'd recite you a long erotic poem in 14th century Japanese, full of 'hong' and 'bong.' Then we'd bow. It would all take hours. We're on the Nippon beat now, you know."

"You're too spirited for a Geisha."

"I could be the one who nabs the Emperor. Shall we ask my aunt Harriet to bring us jasmine tea and use those little cups without handles that the Noh Theatre people gave Dad?"

Bernard watched her with the indulgence, a kind of gratitude, that he had for all actors and most of all for Tam.

"Your aunt's out."

"Damn. There goes my new interpretation. I can't do it without the props," said Tam, shifting comfortably on the desk and grinding up a photograph or two.

8

"Tam, I wish you'd sit in the chair."

"But I like it up here. It's nice to be actually sitting *on* Dad's plans for next season."

He made an involuntary movement and she laughed.

"Relax, relax, I haven't come to steal the secrets. I know them anyway. The big news is that Dad's doing the picture instead of playing the Ibsen."

"He's going to do both."

"That is what he says now," corrected Tam. "But it's the movie he's steamed up about and old Henrik'll have to whistle. Dad's gone off him anyway."

She had the actor's nose for news, and even if Bernard took particular pains to keep some delicate or undecided project quiet, she knew about it the same day.

"I just breathe deeply. It's in the air," she would say, looking bland.

Now she sat, her head on one side, gazing at him thoughtfully.

"So my father's going to produce the picture he's been on about, *and* star in it."

"It isn't signed yet."

"Don't be naïve. It was fixed on Saturday and Dad is taking you with him to look at the location—Sicily, isn't it? I bet that envelope's the air tickets; what else do I know? The director is Clive Diamond, the romantic lead is Peter Moneto; want to hear any more?"

Her expression was uncannily like her father's. She had the same air of lining up the world to make it play "Snap," the same way of slamming down her cards, the same glee in winning. The Warings insisted on winning.

She pulled the pencils from her hair and lightly touched the back of Bernard's hand with one of them.

"If we're not having the Japanese tea ceremony, let's have imperial diplomacy. My date with Dad. You realise it's to-night after supper?"

It didn't seem odd to Tamara that she should make appointments to see her own father. Nowadays Bernard fixed everything. The old routine of flustered secretaries, bullied by Sir Robert, was gone and with Bernard in charge, everything went smoothly. Tam enjoyed conferring with

9

Bernard, fixing things with Bernard. She enjoyed, also, her influence over him.

Bernard had come to the house a year ago to help over a harassing time when Sir Robert was planning a world tour for his Royalty company. His current secretary was on the verge of a breakdown. This was nothing new. He changed secretaries every few months—they fell in love with him and fell into hysterics. Bernard, employed for a fortnight, stayed. At his suggestion the secretary was paid off; sobbing, she got a job at twice the salary. A young girl was hired to type, answer the telephone, and leave at a civilised hour of five-thirty in the evening. It was Bernard who stayed until four in the morning or met Sir Robert at, as it might be, Istanbul. It was Bernard who soothed actors wounded by neglect and wrote letters to ambassadors. He took over the task of organising Sir Robert's working life, and fitted into that life of drama and temperament as if he were an integral part of it. He remained the common-sensical man with a mind of his own, who looked as if he managed a chain of grocers' shops.

After a week or two of behaving coolly to the new arrival and failing to patronise him, Tam accepted him. Later, she welcomed him and he became her ally. She took her disappointments and triumphs to him, crying in his office or putting her arms round his neck and giving him triumphant kisses on the cheek.

Bernard had known for some time that Tam wanted the chance to talk to her father on his own. Between them Bernard and she had fixed that this evening would be the best time.

Tam said with a satisfied sigh :

"I'll *really* be able to talk to him to-night."

Bernard's face clouded.

"Tamara."

She looked so bright and trusting.

"Tamara, he isn't here."

"But he'll be back."

There was a pause.

"I really am sorry," he said, and put out his hand.

Her face altered.

"Where is he? With Clive Diamond?" she said, her voice sharpening.

"He's gone to Paris. He went at lunchtime."

Tam stared at him. He noticed, not for the first time, that she went pale when she was angry: the freckles stood out like pieces of brown confetti on the bridge of her nose.

"He's gone to see Sara de Lullo, the designer," said Bernard.

She was not listening.

"We can easily fix up for you to see him when he gets back in a couple of days——" Bernard went on. But Tam had climbed down from the desk. She gave him a disappointed, furious look and slammed out of the room.

He sighed, pulled his chair to the desk, and began to work.

Muttering "Damn, damn, damn," Tam ran up two flights of stairs to her bedroom, snatched up a leather coat and pulled a suitcase from under her bed.

When Tam wanted something—anything—to do with her work, it was an obsession. She had been like that from the time she joined the Royalty Company from drama school. She cared so passionately about succeeding that for the first few weeks of rehearsing a new play she could scarcely sleep. Tam had inherited her father's ambition; not his marvellous face and not his genius; but she had talent, and a determination to work as strong as sexual passion in another woman. Outwardly fascinating, Tam didn't fall in love. Her affair was with the theatre, her world the international closed society of the drama, her friends were actors, authors, directors, her conversation shop, shop, shop. She didn't want the excitement of a man but the thrill of success, and when she thought it wasn't going right she couldn't bear to talk about it. She couldn't wish another actor luck if her own were in jeopardy.

As daughter of Sir Robert Waring, one of the most famous actors in the world, she'd begun playing in her midteens. Now, at twenty, she'd done well, and all her work, including one or two successes, had been in the Royalty company.

But what Tam wanted all the time was to be where it

was happening, and at present her father was intensely interested in a new film. He'd starred in many in the past, in Hollywood, England and France. This new picture was to be different : he was going to produce as well as play in it. Tam wanted to be in the picture so much that it made her feel sick.

She must talk to him. She never seemed to get the chance. Now and again his sardonic face would look in at her dressing-room door at the Royalty and he'd say "all right?" backing away neatly before she had time to reply. To have her father to herself was essential if she was going to persuade him. She'd planned the day and time with Bernard so carefully—the day, when there was a lull in her father's work; the time, late at night when there were no visitors. This was the only way to win. The demands on her father's time were so heavy that he probably hadn't spared a thought to using Tam in his film. She wanted him to think *now*. He had helped her elder sister Candida to success. Tam considered it was her turn.

Candida had become an "instant star," as the newspapers had called her, two years ago in her father's production of Chekhov's *The Cherry Orchard*. Critics and audiences had fallen in love with her. Now she was away filming in America, and although Tam missed her sister, the present situation had advantages. Without a brilliant elder around, "Sir" must concentrate on Tam.

The airport was crowded, and it was not until her flight number was called and she joined the queue of passengers boarding the plane that she felt a qualm over Bernard. Would he be in trouble for having told her where her father had gone, and being, in part, responsible for her sudden appearance in Paris? She felt a little guilty at leaving him without saying good-bye. Tam had the female reaction to a man strongly attracted to her but for whom she felt only affection : a tender patronage. "Poor Bernard." But she continued to make sure her spell over him went on working.

The plane roared and was airborne and Tam thought of Bernard toiling away below in London. "He's one of the family," she thought sentimentally as she left him behind.

The fact was that nobody could work closely with her father unless he joined the family. Only a man dedicated to the star and the drama, one and the same thing as far as Robert Waring was concerned, could succeed. Bernard's working hours were his waking hours; from the time the telephone rang well in advance of his alarm clock at home, to the time he returned to his flat (where Robert Waring telephoned as he put his key in the lock) Bernard's life belonged to the Warings. Tam approved. Bernard's devotion to her father was a symbol of the world. He'd been taken over by the great mesmerist. You were taken over or thrown over, there were no half measures with Sir.

Tam also had an idea that Bernard was in love with her; he had a trick of remembering her likes and dislikes, of quoting her words. Once she'd called him her "teddy bear." It was the only time she'd seen him angry.

"I meant it as a compliment!" she'd protested.

"If you can't manage anything better, then shut up."

She undid her seat belt and forgot about Bernard. Now that the journey had started, and every minute brought her nearer what she wanted so hungrily, she allowed herself time to admire the sunset, something she hadn't managed to do with the michaelmas daisies in the garden at home.

The air hostess came round for orders for drinks. There was a stir beside her, and a voice said :

"Won't you have some champagne with me?"

Tam raised her eyebrows.

The man lounging in the seat beside her was about twenty-seven or twenty-eight, with the bright red hair that children nickname "carrots." He had blue eyes with dark lashes and a big mouth.

"Do say yes," he said matily. "A nice glass of ice cold champagne."

"Thank you, no."

Her voice should have closed the conversation but the man continued to look both cheerful and confident. He put his hands in his pockets, and stared at the toes of his shabby shoes.

"Champagne, please," he said to the air hostess. She, at least, had the conscious air of a woman with an attractive

13

man. When he said : "I leave the brand to you : just choose an expensive one," she simpered.

When she'd gone he spoke to Tam again.

"Can't I persuade you to change your mind? It's depressing to drink alone; and I deserve that champagne."

There was a pause during which she was meant to ask why.

She opened a magazine.

"Every sold computers?" he inquired.

"No."

She lifted the paper close to her face as if she were short-sighted.

"It's no joke, believe me," he said, addressing his remarks to the magazine cover which said in bold black letters : "The Disappearing Virgins of London—inside."

"The way for a salesman to succeed is to show the customer a sample. You'd agree to that, wouldn't you? Can't do that with a computer. It needs a hotel suite. Computers are Britain's next housing problem—central heating, sound-proofing, no vibrations, room to expand, they need the lot. I knew one so heavy it fell right through the first floor of a bank. You can't send them by freight; they get ill. Another computer of my acquaintance, quite an old friend, was convinced it was on fire all the time. Kept sending signals to the local fire station. We told it that it wasn't on fire—it just wouldn't believe us. Of course . . ." he went on ruminatively, "if you ever do sell one you're doing all right; they cost hundreds of thousands. I've never managed it. Hence the champagne."

Tam listened to this long speech from behind her paper with growing irritation. She disliked fending off males, and was not often in the situation of having to do so. The men she went around with were actors. They enjoyed talking about themselves and their roles; they rarely made a play for her, and never if she didn't want it.

She put The Disappearing Virgins of London down and ostentatiously closed her eyes.

A moment later there was a cheerful "pop!" of a cork and some jokes from the air hostess.

Tam remained with her eyes shut.

14

Her companion did not speak again, and she lay and listened to the engines taking her towards Paris.

After a time she noticed a stillness beside her, and cautiously opened her eyes. He really was asleep. A second glass of champagne, sadly festive, stood untouched on a plastic tray.

Safe from the assault of friendliness, she looked at him rather curiously. He was handsome in an uneven flamboyant way; his nose had a big bump in its centre, and in sleep he frowned. His thick pale skin, freckled like her own, was the texture which sunburns and blushes. Tam didn't think he looked like a salesman. In movies and plays they never left a drink, but swallowed one down after another and shouted for more. The matey manner, of course, was right. But not the white, frowning face.

She wondered how she'd cast him in a play; it was a game she played now and then. He would win in a wrestling match, like Orlando, but could she imagine him writing bad verses and pinning them on trees? Perhaps he'd be better drinking and fooling with Falstaff? Studying the sleeping man, she thought it had been absurd of her to have been so cold. But the next minute she forgot him, and returned to thinking about her father's film, and her urgent desire to play in it.

The sky had faded to a clear deep blue when Tam drove through Paris, and the wind that had blown lime leaves across the Hampstead lawn was pulling conkers from the trees in the Tuileries.

The taxi stopped at the Hotel de Noailles, a 17th century building, once a palace, on a corner of the Place de la Concorde. The glass doors of the hotel worked by ray, and as Tam approached they swung open on to a foyer where a fire burned in a high, marble fireplace. The Noailles fire was familiar to Tam; it burned all winter long, night and day. Sometimes in the past, when she'd crossed Concorde in the dark, she had seen the fire glowing, from the other side of the huge square. It shone through the glass doors, a beacon of luxury.

Tam had known the hotel since she was a child: her father always stayed there and she didn't bother to check

15

at Reception. The porters would automatically tell her he was in conference. One particular porter with rimless glasses and a shaved grey head was capable of stopping her from going to her father's suite until he'd first telephoned for permission : daughters in France still kept their place. The Noailles' reverence for Sir Robert went, Tam considered, to idiotic lengths. "The French understand an artist," her father would say, when seventeen members of the staff, looking like a contingent from an imperial palace guard, trooped out to bid him goodbye.

The foyer was covered with thick crimson carpet woven with Napoleon's cypher, the laurel-wreathed "N." Tam waded through this, avoided the porters and slipped up the staircase. She went down a long hot corridor smelling of coffee and central heating to a pair of doors she knew very well indeed. Sure enough, as she approached, a voice reverberated :

"Everybody will disagree, and then I shall come along and settle everything!"

Tam opened the doors quietly and peered into the room, exactly as she had done this afternoon to Bernard.

Her father was seated in a high-backed velvet chair, his legs crossed, and the table in front of him spread with costume designs. He wore a dark suit, the narrow ribbon of the Croix de Guerre in his buttonhole. At forty-eight, Robert Waring was still the most fascinating actor in the world. He had high cheek bones, lustrous eyes and a tough, expressive mouth. His figure was powerful and slender; body and manner were both controlled, as if by a rider managing a high-spirited horse. He did nothing by mistake.

When Tam put her head round the door he looked up. His large eyes gleamed. He said nothing.

"You might at least be *surprised*," she said, coming in with a slight swagger.

"We are never surprised. Sometimes displeased. What are you doing here?"

"Just popped over." Her face fell with anti-climax.

"Indeed," drawled her father. "Sara, this is my daughter Tamara. Tamara, this is Miss Sara de Lullo who is a very

16

brilliant designer," he added in a tone of instruction. It was a habit of her father's to indicate to Tam whom she should show regard for, and a maddennig habit it was, since she was extremely quick and did not need to be nudged.

Sara de Lullo was fiftyish, with a weather-beaten, blissful face and large spectacles. She smiled and returned to the designs.

Tam found herself standing in the middle of the room, like an actress held up at rehearsal.

Her father folded his arms and looked her up and down.

"I take it that my production of *As You* is not in the repertory to-night?"

"Really, Dad! You don't think I'd come over to Paris if I had a performance!"

"If it suited your book, you'd come over and miss half a dozen performances, having fixed with the stage director, by giving my invented permission. Take off that religious expression. Since you are here, you may dine with me to-night and I will see you back on a plane later to-night."

"Dad!"

Ignoring the wail, he lifted the telephone, ordered a plane reservation in flowing French.

"Now pick up your suitcase and go and have a bath while Sara and I finish our work."

Tam left the room meekly.

His suggestion that she should pass the time while she waited by having a bath was typical. Dad was always deciding what people should do while they waited . . . and they waited for him all the time. When Tam was fifteen, he had sent her to the British Museum to find the shape of sandals worn in Ancient Crete, and made her telephone the Botanical Gardens to check the colour of an orchid. Once she'd spent a whole day drawing him a sketch map of 15th century London.

Tam adored her father, was amused and fascinated by him, too much under his thumb. It had not always been like that.

The girls' mother had died when they were children. Tam had been a baby, and the Waring family, Robert, his half-sister Harriet, and the elder girl Candida, had petted Tam. She was "little puss." She grew up in an atmosphere of demonstrative love, for actors show their feelings; she knew, when she ran into a room, she would as like as not be kissed. Her family's indulgent love had been a sort of wall against which Tam leaned with comfort, a wall which started to collapse the day she started to act. Acting was hard and you were on your own. Her family encouraged her, her father took her into the Royalty company, even the critics—touched by the Waring look—were kind. Tam was on her own just the same. Her self-confidence with her father collapsed the first, and Tam began to see him differently. Candida still defied and coaxed him, and even refused to be an actress for a time. But Tam did everything she was told.

"I can't manage him any more," she thought, obediently going into the bathroom at the Noailles and turning on the taps.

Her father's bathroom at the hotel was one of Tam's favourite places : it was pompous. Designed in 1900, proud of it, and decorated to look like a Persian palace, it had acanthus tiles of blue and grey, and taps shaped like the heads of lions. When she turned them, scalding rusty water gushed out, as it had always done. The towels were embroidered with the Napoleonic "N," and were enormous; the spotted mirror was held in place by stout cupids.

Tam took a long time to dress, doing her hair two or three times and spending particular care on her eyes, using a thick and thin paintbrush. When she was ready, she looked at herself in the mirror with approval.

Back in the salon, Sara de Lullo had gone and her father was alone. Newly-changed into a white silk shirt and black silk suit, he was smoking a thin cigar and reading *Figaro*.

He put down the paper.

"Let me look at you."

She came across the room, switching on the radiance that actors use, an electric beam of poise. She was wearing a dress of greenish blue, and a thick gold bracelet her father had brought from Finland.

18

"The eye make-up's been put on with a trowel but we'll let you get away with it for this evening. Give your father a kiss."

They embraced and she sat down on his knee. He put an arm round her waist and continued to smoke.

"So you've come for a part in the picture."

The careless tone and perfect accuracy made her start so much that she nearly fell off his knee. He laughed.

"Up you get. It's no good playing the Victorian miss sitting on Papa's lap. Sit on a chair while I talk to you."

Discomfited, she drew up a spindly chair facing him. He looked at her with eyebrows slightly raised. Tam knew that look; it presaged somebody—Tam herself—not getting her own way. She looked brightly back, hiding dismay.

Her father had been away in Greece and he was as tanned as a Red Indian. The brown skin enhanced his high cheek bones and slanting eyes. His face, mask-like, closed, was impossible to read. Was he the autocrat? The loving parent? The tease? Tam had no idea.

"Come along. Say what you've come over to Paris to say."

She went scarlet.

"I'm waiting . . ."

"I won't! I won't beg!" she exclaimed, the blush spreading to her forehead. "It's bad enough having to come over here—why, it's ridiculous! What other girl has to make appointments with her own father, which he never keeps either . . . And lately it's been getting worse!"

"Of course it has."

"You mean you think you should see less of me now that I'm an adult!" she cried. "You *prefer* not to see your children!"

She sprang up because it was easier to be angry when walking about. "Last week I waited a whole day to talk to you . . . and in the end I never got the chance . . . and when I complained to Bernard he was so harassed I could have strangled him! I don't care how busy you are——"

"Bravo!"

"What I care about is being given the chance to talk to my own father when I need to."

19

Robert Waring had been listening with a sceptical air. When she finished she sat down heavily on the chair, which creaked loudly. He glanced at the chair with interest.

A pause.

"Is that all?"

"Yes it is!"

He drew on his cigar.

"Very well. Let us begin with your complaint that I am busier than I used to be. True. The Royalty is expanding. We have foreign tours, regional tours, experimental work . . . and as it gets more complex, so it needs more of me. You know all that, Tamara. Perfectly well.

"As for the role of outraged daughter, it just doesn't work. Are you actually saying I would be too busy for you if you needed me? You don't need fatherly help. You want something very different. To wheedle a part out of me, in exactly the same way as every other actress in the business. If you wanted to talk about anything but work——"

"What is there——" she began involuntarily, and was answered by a roar of laughter. Furious with herself, she couldn't help laughing too.

"Tamara, Tamara, I don't need to ask where you get that reaction from. It's curious to see it repeated in another human being . . . especially one so much younger and *shorter* than I. I knew you'd want the part in *Tempest 72*. You've noticed it's a very nice part. And so have a lot of actresses."

"Dad!"

The desperate tone pleased him. He put his hands on either side of her face and stared down at her. "Miranda," he said reflectively, "sexy, teenage Miranda. Think you could do it? We'll see . . . we'll see . . ."

He continued to study his daughter's face.

*

The taxi crawled down a narrow street on the Ile de la Cité beside a river wall and trees overlooking the water. Along one side of the street was a row of pinkish-grey houses, many with plaques: "Ici demeurait le chirurgien du Roi Louis XIII," "Le Comte de la Tour . . ."

"They chopped off their nobility's heads and have been boasting ever since about the ones that are left. Why don't

20

the French make up their mind what they do think is important," said Tam, after reading the plaques aloud.

"The French are a well-balanced nation who know exactly what is important."

"You mean they've always adored you and say you're the greatest in the world."

"So I am and you pipe down."

The taxi stopped at a modest-seeming restaurant. Tam, climbing from the car, exclaimed with pleasure. To-night she admired everything (except the French, of course). She liked the river, so clean that men still fished in it, the lovers kissing under a tree, the houses pressing together in the dusk . . . the words: "Think you could do it?" which her father had spoken. Those, most of all.

The restaurant had the low-key look of expensive places: the furniture had been in a farmhouse in the 18th century and was polished like glass; a painting of ogling girls was by Renoir. The tiled floor, embroidered carpets, welcomed them in low voices. The air smelled of spices.

The maître d'hotel came over to welcome them. In the *Michelin Guide* this restaurant was awarded three stars, the highest in a rigid score of excellence; Tam decided the maître d'hotel's welcoming bows were graded as well, and her father was given the deepest.

When they were seated at a corner table, her father looked over at her with amusement.

"Happy?"

"Yes!"

"Think you can play the part?"

"Yes!"

"It needs technique to be innocent without being wet."

"*I know!*"

He laughed at the intense voice. Indulgence had replaced his edged manner of earlier this evening, and Tam thought how delicious this evening was.

"Dad," she said. "Why is this a table for three?"

"Because that's how many we are going to be."

"Is Sara de Lullo coming?" she said, disappointed.

"Guess again."

Before she could reply, the waiter came up to give her

father the menu. Food was discussed at length. The waiter talked of the dishes for which the restaurant was famous ... lobster with vermouth, lamb with rosemary sprigs burned crisp on the outsides, potatoes flavoured with cognac.

Tam fidgeted. The moment the waiter had left she said: "Who's coming? I don't want to share you with anyone."

"That's nice," he said quizzically.

"Who *is* it?"

"Somebody you are going to know rather well, I imagine. And here he comes."

Across the room came a man with bright red hair, the kind that children nickname "carrots." It was the computer salesman.

"Tamara, this is David Bryden, the author of *Tempest 72*," said her father, nudging her with his voice for the second time that evening. "David, my daughter, who much admires your work. She's only over for the evening, by the way, to enjoy the food and listen to our conversation."

Tam waited for the young man to mention their meeting. But he shook hands with her, giving her the inattentive glance that Sara de Lullo had done: the look people gave everybody but Sir when he was present.

"I'm sorry I'm late, I was hiring a car and I had to wait. I'm driving to Fontainebleau to-morrow."

"That's all right, we haven't missed you! What will you drink?"

David Bryden didn't reply but started immediately:

"I've been working on the first island sequence, the one Clive wants rejigged, and the idea just won't do. It won't do at all."

The waiter came up with the menu. David waved it impatiently aside as if being offered fish and chips and said "that'll be fine" without ordering anything. He continued to talk.

"Prospero can't be with the comics when my whole point was to make him stay alone——"

"But we already told you——"

"I know what you're going to say," interrupted David before her father could finish the sentence. "The camera will do it for me. It won't. No amount of arty hand-held film

22

is going to work when the audience damn well doesn't know what's happening!"

"My dear boy——"

The men settled down to talk. Her father was dismissive. David refused to be dismissed. The talk was about fictional characters and their fictional motives, and it could only interest people involved with the invisible creatures. But Tam had read the play over and over; she had also seen it at the Royal Court, where it had been given interested, picky notices and run for a few weeks. It had been a play with a brief appearance and a reputation that continued to grow, a thing that happens sometimes. It came into the news again when Robert Waring announced he was producing it as a film.

Tam was fascinated by the play, and as an actress who had grown up on Shakespeare, saw that the writer had been daring. He'd based the work on Shakespeare's *Tempest*, using the same characters in a modern world. Adapting Shakespeare to to-day wasn't new; it had been done in *West Side Story* and in *Rosencrantz and Guildenstern Are Dead*. But David had interpolated quite long scenes from Shakespeare into his work, a risk few writers would dare to take, following these with scenes of his own. It shouldn't have worked but it did. Somebody called *Tempest 72* a piece of counterpoint to genius.

Some of Robert Waring's financier friends warned him about the proposed picture: it could lose money. The play hadn't succeeded, so why should it work as a movie? But when Robert Waring had a strong instinct about a piece of work, sound advice from men of business left him unmoved; he would listen with great courtesy and do the exact opposite. He and Clive Diamond believed *Tempest 72* could make a dazzling film. When one of his richest and shrewdest friends in the City again raised the question of financial success, he replied simply:

"Who's starring in it? And who brings the cash into the box office?"

Now, as Tam ate her dinner and listened to her father and David Bryden talking about the film, she waited to hear her own name as a possible Miranda. Half an hour

23

went by. Her father didn't say a word about it. Her good spirits began to flag as she realised that it could be days, or even weeks before she knew that the part was hers. Her father hadn't made up his mind after all. A producer of a film was like a juggler keeping numbers of balls in the air at once; there was the money, the director, the actors he particularly wanted, the right timing, the place. All in the air. And so was she.

The meal, exquisitely cooked and served, went on a long time; her father and Bryden ate it and talked. The wine was 30 years old and tasted of flowers; they drank it and talked. Coffee was served in an earthenware pot that looked as if Picasso had made it. They talked on. And she began to understand why her father hadn't said she might get the role. For the man who'd joked with her on the plane was not what he seemed. At times euphoric, at times argumentative, he was restless and nervy; he was the only man she'd seen with her father who contradicted him flatly. Tam was slightly shocked; she was accustomed to her father getting respectful, often rapt, attention. But to-night Robert Waring didn't use any weight in counter-attack, and avoided his speciality : the jaw-dropping sarcasm. He merely chuckled. Tam decided she rather disliked Bryden for other reasons. Perhaps because he'd played a foolish trick on her. Or was it because he ignored her?

Once again Bryden exclaimed : "No, no, Sir, you are *wrong*!" He gulped wine as if it were cocoa, and shook his head so vigorously that his hair jumped up on his head.

"Well, we'll have to go on with this in the morning, won't we?" said Robert Waring. He looked at his watch. "Gentle heavens, Puss, you must go. I can't have you missing that plane. Have you enjoyed yourself?"

"The food was delicious," she said.

He did not miss the inflection, and gave her a sly glance.

"I have to go to the Comédie Française to see some pals after the performance. David, boy, could you drive my daughter to Le Bourget for me?"

"That's not necessary. I'll get a cab," said Tam.

"I'll be glad to take her," said David, looking up from

doodling on the tablecloth. Tam was just about to refuse again when her father bustled her to her feet.

"Good, good, then we must hurry. I don't want you staying the night in Paris, that wouldn't do at all. It might encourage you to pop over again."

Conscious and unconscious of the looks that people gave him as he walked across the restaurant, he shepherded them into the street. It was cold and there was a mist.

"Don't let your *As You* performance suffer because I gave you a nice dinner or I shall hear about it," he said, kissing her.

She put her arms round him and hugged him. She could hear, as he pressed her close, a voiceless command to say nothing to David about why she had come.

"I won't be home for the rest of the week. Tell Bernard I'll be in touch and kiss your aunt for me," he said.

As David drove her away, Tam looked back and saw her father striding off under the trees.

Beneath the Arc de Triomphe a great tricolour was billowing in the night wind, and the red tail lights of cars ahead of them made a thick band of rubies. Cinemas large as palaces stood on either side of the avenue.

"Dad's film will be shown in one of those. Will I be in it?" thought Tam.

"I love French movie posters, don't you?" remarked David. "I never recognise our films from the French versions. They have a go and it comes out all different."

They were driving past a poster of a giant girl with bulbous breasts and legs ten yards long, wearing white lace panties and looking alarmed. A man in a dinner suit leered hopefully over her shoulder.

"Le Sexy. Thirty years behind the times," he said.

He had apparently decided to ignore their meeting on the plane.

"Why a computer salesman?" she said baldly.

He smiled.

"That's what I used to be as a matter of fact. I thought it a good starter for a chat. It's always slightly funny to recognise somebody when they don't recognise you."

She was embarrassed. In the theatre, not to know somebody was the sure way to hurt them.

"Of course I saw *Tempest 72* and I've read all your work . . ."

"You must think me stupid if you imagine I care whether I'm recognised or not," he said, quite mildly.

She was irritated again.

"Why shouldn't you care? It's part of the thing we do."

"It's part of what you do. It is my words, not my face, that I hope they'll know. And I've talked too much about those to-night. I'm sure I was boring as hell."

She made a murmur of denial.

They were driving down a boulevard edged with faded trees and cobbled so that the car shuddered. It was a shabby street, with stretches of unkempt pavement and tumble-down shops; here and there was a small petrol station, locked and dark, and they passed the walls of a gaol, through the windows of which were lights gleaming as dim as gaslight.

Tam was glad when the car turned at a busy junction, went down a concrete slipway blazing with neon and out on to the Autoroute. The car crept to seventy and David drove in silence.

Tam's thoughts turned to her father, walking across Paris. He enjoyed walking at night. He would arrive at the Comédie Française to be warmly welcomed, actresses would kiss him on both cheeks and entertain him in dressing-rooms where Molière had once sat. Dad always made good jokes in good French. Later he would walk back to the Noailles, deep in his own thoughts. She envied him his freedom. The young man beside her also had some of that male liberty.

The car drew to a stop at the front of the airport, and David climbed out to open the door for her. She thanked him brightly. "Don't bother to see me off," she added, in the voice of a woman sure that he would.

"Oh, would you prefer that?" he said, looking down at her seriously, "I know how you feel; I like being alone myself. Good night. Have a good flight. Don't talk to any salesmen!"

He drove away without looking back.

*

It was two days after her trip to Paris and the weather was still sunny, the sky full of bowling white clouds. It was an *As You Like It* day, the play was performed both at the matinee and evening performance, so that the sets did not have to be changed twice in a day. *As You Like It* is always a favourite, and this production was still three-quarters full after months in the repertory.

When the matinee was over, Tam walked out of the Stage Door. Three 15-year-olds were waiting, two girls and a boy. Tam signed their autographs, wishing there had been a hundred. She set off down the street, walking with a swing. She was on her way to meet Bernard.

He had forgiven her for rushing over to Paris without telling him; and had merely said "Why didn't you tell me? I could have driven you to the Airport."

He hadn't asked how her meeting with her father had gone, or whether she was any nearer getting her desired part. Used to actors, Bernard knew that if Tam didn't tell it was because she was worried.

The player resembles a little animal called the shrew who must eat every half hour or die. With an actor it is not food and money that are necessary to life but work. Of course the actor needs money to live by, and of course he welcomes more because it is a symbol that he is a success. But what nourishes him is acting, actually doing it; doing it every day and night, and being offered more and more work, with greater strains and stresses.

Tam ran up the steps of the Ritz and through the rooms, which with their French style and looking-glasses reminded her of the Noailles.

Bernard was in the Rivoli bar, reading the *Evening Standard*. Looking over at him, Tam thought that Bernard, with his fattish body and square clothes and short hair and taste for indeterminate grey, was the only man in the theatre who looked as if he was nothing to do with it. It was astonishing that Sir should even interview a man who wore huge heavy shoes, polished like a guardsman's.

"Tam!" He sprang up.

27

He asked her what she would like to drink. She chose carrot juice, which she disliked and believed controlled the imaginary double chin.

She opened her handbag and looked at herself in a little glass, flicking a lock of hair across her forehead. She was wearing a yellow leather coat and a dress the colour of toffee, both chosen to enhance her hair. The actress uses her appearance, not to please men or herself, but to show that she *is* an actress. She makes it impossible for people not to look at her, and bathes in the attention she has silently commanded as if it is her personal ultra-violet lamp.

When Bernard had reacted as he should, with a look of admiration, and so had both the barmen, and a girl and a man on a settee nearby, Tam settled down to gossip.

Bernard talked about the Royalty's coming season, the foreign companies who were visiting the theatre for a fortnight each, including the Chinese State Theatre. Had Tam heard about the forty-foot-long dragon which was to be used, and which went right through the stalls and past the box office? They discussed the coming film, both avoiding the subject of Miranda, and behaving as if there were no role for a young actress in the picture.

"Did I tell you David Bryden dined with Dad and me in Paris?" said Tam.

"Sir mentioned it. I hear Bryden's having a success in the French theatre. They're doing *Tempest 72* at the T.N.P.," said Bernard.

Tam was annoyed at not knowing this. It occurred to her that she had not been very clever with David Bryden.

"Why haven't we done a play of his at the Royalty?" she said.

"Why indeed."

Bernard sounded sour and she was intrigued.

"He's much admired, isn't he? Dad's got 72, and the French are doing it. But I thought I heard the Royal Shakespeare Company have nabbed his next play. We ought to have it."

"He wouldn't give it to us."

"Ha ha."

"It's true, Tamara. He turned us down."

"But authors never turn my father down!"

"Apparently nobody told Bryden that."

Bernard laughed at her gaping face, and her surrender to her father as the despot and genius who never made a mistake.

"Sir's relationship with David Bryden can scarcely be classed as a failure," he said. "He's got *Tempest 72*. It's a heaven-sent chance for the company to play Shakespeare and new work together. It's all fine. Isn't it?"

"But to say no to Dad!" said Tam, still astonished. "What's David Bryden like really. Didn't you work with him once?"

"Yes. Before I came to work for Sir. It was on David's first play at Doncaster. He was okay. Rather good, as a matter of fact. Energetic and nervous and funny. He likes jokes. He was very moody, I remember, and had ideas that you just couldn't budge. I agree that creative people ought to be stubborn on occasions, but it can also be a bit of a bore. One way and another, he's a writer you can't ignore."

Tam said she knew what he meant.

"You know how a writer can lose command when he gets inside a theatre," Bernard said reflectively. "You and I have both seen it happen at the Royalty. Directors are inclined to bully authors—some authors, anyway. It's the same in TV. Some of the writers are treated like people manufacturing sausages. At Doncaster it wasn't like that often, but we had a clever young director who really was a bully. He used to re-write chunks of an author's work— write it himself, and very badly too. Then Bryden arrived."

"What happened?"

"One argument and Bryden knocked him down."

"Oh no!" exclaimed Tam. Her father had once punched a critic on the jaw; it was a favourite story.

"Anyone we know?" she asked.

"My dear girl, that director's now quite a distinguished man. I doubt if he, or David either, would like it known."

"Why not?" asked Tam, much amused.

"Punching people on the jaw isn't a sign of strength of

mind, Tamara, as David Bryden knows quite well," said Bernard in the tone Tam found annoying when he used it, rather reproving, rather schoolmasterish.

When they had finished their drinks, he took her back to the theatre in a taxi. At the Stage Door they passed Sid, the stage doorkeeper, who was reading the racing results with the paper folded small. He had been sitting in the same cubbyhole for 20 years doing just that. He waved at them with the indifference he used to great names as well as walk-ons.

They went up the narrow stone stairway of the theatre to the dressing-rooms. Tam shared hers with two other actresses in the company, and the room was bursting with costumes of brown and dark yellow, orange and saffron. The *As You* production was set in autumn and not in spring. Wigs, stays, shoes with tongues and buckles, white cotton stockings, petticoats of coarse buckram, were neatly ranged. Tam, like her father and sister, was one of the first players in the theatre before a performance; she needed a long time to herself. The room was empty.

Bernard lingered, his hands in his pockets, as Tam took off her coat and looked for messages. She liked writing notes, which she left propped on dressing-tables, and enjoyed even more receiving them. There was nothing for her this evening and she was disappointed. As she broke a dead flower off some long-stemmed gladioli on her dressing-table, the glaring lights reflected her face. Bernard stood watching her. She was like a new-minted penny, unused and bright so that you didn't want it to be spent. She was like fine weather seen through a window-pane. There was something shiny and heartless about her. Bernard knew Tam was selfish and ambitious, with her eye on the main chance. As the young Waring girl, he considered these qualities in her were perfectly suitable. Tam used him; why shouldn't she? Her nervous egoism touched him as much as her round, pale-ish face and the timbre of her voice. Bernard saw Tam, as he saw her father, surrounded with a sort of light.

She looked up, caught his eyes on her and came across the room to him, taking him by his elbows and standing on tiptoe.

"Give us a kiss. You're a darling and I adore you."

"And I know what that means!" he said.

*

Tam thought the audience that night was heavy and flat. Members of the company, coming offstage, shuddered as if emerging from cold water. When an audience was like that, Tam always found herself inwardly addressing them : "Why aren't you doing it, you can! Why are you keeping yourselves from us?"

She had refused an invitation to supper that evening. Most of the company saw each other morning, noon and night; there was always someone giving a party or a scratch meal, meeting for drinks or coffee. Just now, Tam would rather be alone.

Her father's black Rolls was waiting to collect her in the square near the Stage Door. At one time he had made Tam and her sister Candida travel to and from the theatre by bus, while he bowled past them in his car. But Candida's success had made this difficult; people recognised her; and after both girls had been squeezed off bus seats by admiring males, Robert Waring allowed them his car. Cars of their own he banned, saying that he wasn't having any more cars on the road if he could help it. Even two.

Tam was glad to hunch herself in the corner of the car and stare out of the window as she was driven home. Her father's chauffeur, usually given to chat, was silent. When they arrived, she went hastily indoors.

She was lonely and hungry and hurried towards the kitchen, looking for her aunt, who usually waited with her supper. Tam loved Harriet, her father's half-sister, and to-night felt in need of her practical, warm company. But the kitchen was empty. There was a message on the table.

"Sorry, darling, gone to the ballet. There's a new one that sounds terrible. Turkey in oven, soufflé in frig, soup in thermos. Don't eat in kitchen, Dad doesn't like it. Luv H."

Tam sighed. She poured some soup into a mug, pulled up a stool to the table, and cradled the mug in her hands. It was too hot to drink. She had thought she was hungry, but she didn't want to eat. She was lonely, too, but being

31

alone didn't matter. She could only think of her father's promise. A half promise. Worse than nothing at all.

Suppose he changed his mind? He often did. In the *As You* production he had recast the role of Orlando a few days before the opening because the actor previously chosen hadn't been right. It was hard on the first boy, a friend of Tam's, who was sacked overnight. Her father often brooded over casting for weeks and then made lightning decisions, most of which hurt somebody.

She put down the mug and went abruptly out of the kitchen.

The house was quiet and dark, a single light shone at the foot of the stairs, and the grandfather clock whirred and struck—eleven o'clock. This was the house she'd known since she was born; it could spring into life and light, fill with people, and empty again like a huge bath. It was a theatre as well as a home. But to-night it was only a shell of dark, smelling of chrysanthemums.

Tam trailed up the stairs.

She looked automatically along the landing towards her father's door and, to her surprise, saw a line of light. Bernard must be working late again. Glad that her friend was in the house, she slapped open the door:

"Idiot! Sir never pays overtime!"

"Doesn't he, though?"

She stood in the doorway, blinking.

"Dad! Why aren't you in Paris?"

"Daughter! Why are you discussing my staff's pay?"

"A joke, a joke," she said hastily.

"Jokes that create the desire for more money in my staff don't get a laugh with me. Sit down. The *As You* audience was bloody to-night, I gather."

"Were you in front——"

"I only came off the plane thirty minutes ago," he said, looking at her sideways. He enjoyed taking people by surprise; he never tired of playing conjuror.

The room was warm, a fire crackled noisily, fresh-lit, and he walked over to throw on a log, which gave a spurt of sparks. He turned, with his hand on the chimney piece, to look at her.

32

He was dressed in a dark blue robe given him by one of his friends in the Indian theatre. The robe was woven by hand, it was uneven and stiff with gold thread, had a high collar and loose sleeves. It was shortish, and his legs were bare. He wore soft black leather sandals. He often changed into these clothes when he worked at night: they were comfortable and unconstricted. They also made any other male around look like a unit in a population chart.

He sat down on the settee and patted the cushion beside him. As she went over she met his eyes and thought: "They're too clever."

"Stop worrying about yourself," he said.

"I can't help it."

"No, you can't. You're not like your sister. You let it eat you. Be its master."

"It's all very well for——"

"All very well," he repeated, dropping his jaw with an expression of exaggerated amazement. "All very well? It is never very well. Work needs patience and thought and philosophy. A bit of guile. And will power," he added, clenching one fist. He examined the fist and unclenched it again.

"There is also the matter of a sense of fun, and I'll thank you to take that pious look off your face, Tamara. I am not dealing with a 16th century nun who sees visions. Shall I tell you what you've been doing since that little escapade of yours to Paris? It illustrates my point . . . you've been off your food but sleeping like a log. You've seen a bit of Bernard. You've given a couple of indifferent performances as Audrey in my production. And now at home, having left your supper, you're muttering to yourself like that nun at a litany, that if Dad doesn't give you the part in his picture you'll die!"

She didn't enjoy being laughed at; still less being perfectly interpreted. She wanted him to admire, not to goad her.

"Tamara, I told you we'd see about the part. It is time you began to film. Movies give an actor another dimension. On stage we act mainly from here . . ." he said, indicating his mouth. "In films, we play from here . . ." and in the air his fingers circled his large eyes. "Making a film should be good for you. A nice little part——"

"Not so little."

"Large enough," he said, showing his teeth in a grin. "Let's put you out of your misery. The part is yours. No, no, girl, don't choke me. I have another surprise. The schedule's moved forward because of the weather. We're afraid the leaves will be off the trees if we don't get a move on. We're going on location at the end of this week!"

*

For the next few days, the house at Hampstead was full of visitors. Tam was used to seeing members of the Royalty management around, she'd known most of them for years. The film people were new. From quarter to eight in the morning until midnight, men arrived and drove away, were given drinks and meals, could be heard laughing, or observed walking with Sir Robert round the garden, apparently being shown the michaelmas daisies.

Tam was stimulated by the newcomers, although she had not met any of them yet. Some represented money, and these looked to her unimpressive and mild. She peered out of the window one afternoon and said to her aunt: "It is annoying rich men don't look rich."

"Those aren't the ones with the cash. Just representatives."

"Still, a bit of vulgarity would be nice," Tam said.

Actors, on the other hand, were instantly recognisable.

Her aunt did not enjoy the bustle as Tam did, and remained laconic.

One afternoon she came into the kitchen and found her niece sitting on the table, accompanied by an actor's daughter from the company, whose name was Alexey. Alexey was thirteen, had green eyes, and adored Tam, listening to everything she said with an intense brightness.

"Who's the man hanging about in the hall? He's a new one. He has pop eyes," Harriet said to Tam, fetching some chocolate biscuits which she offered, without comment, to a gratified Alexey.

"When I asked him what he wanted, he just glared and said he'd been called," she added.

34

"Perhaps he's a missionary," suggested Alexey.

Tam giggled.

"Maybe there's a meeting of focus pullers, and he's their leader," she suggested.

"Spare me the gibberish. Sir has not told me of any meetings at which anybody has been called. Ah well. Bread and butter is never unwelcome."

Harriet went into the larder to fetch a big loaf.

Robert Waring's half-sister had been a ballet dancer when she was young, and still had a dancer's look. Her leg muscles were over-developed, she wore heelless slippers, and walked with a flat-footed toes-out movement, like an ageing Degas figure. Her olive-coloured face was worn, her expression rather haunting. Her brother sometimes said she was a tragic muse, at other times a dead-pan who should be in American movies.

"There's always a part for you in comedies. You're the not-so-young woman friend," he'd say. "You get the best lines."

She had a quiet voice and a brief manner. Her grey hair was worn in a severe bob, and she was rarely seen out of a white overall with the sleeves rolled up. Her life was spent on her brother and his daughters. She had looked after them from the time Robert Waring's wife had died, insisted on the job of housekeeper, and could never be coaxed from the family to backstage.

"I can actually see *through* your bread and butter," Alexey said, holding up a piece to the light, "I came to tea once, and there was a breeze and my bit floated right off the plate into the garden."

"We ought to put it in an art show. Objet trouvé," added Tam. Harriet was too late to stop Tam from following Alexey and eating two slices.

"One hundred and ten calories," she said.

Tam groaned.

"Why don't you lock me out of the kitchen? It's awful being with people of thirteen, they're encouraged to *eat*. Harry, I've remembered who the man in the hall is. Bernard said they're having a story conference, so he must be a bit of that. Shall I go and look through the keyhole?"

35

"No. Go and ask Bernard how many for tea and mind you get the number right. And you, Alexey, ought to be off home doing that project you're always bragging about."

Alexey, with regret, left the kitchen, and Tam ran upstairs to Bernard's office.

"Harry says when and where and how many for tea and you've deeply offended her by not letting her know," she said, bursting into Bernard's room because she knew her father to be somewhere else.

Bernard immediately looked worried.

"It's nice kidding you," she said. "You're so easy to take in. Harry's not annoyed. Just making officious mutters. Anyway, what's happening? There's a man in the hall with pop eyes."

"He's the script supervisor. Sir says he has goitre and ought to get it seen to," said Bernard. He and Tam went out into the passage, and he added in a low voice, "I had to stop Sir from having a long medical chat with the poor chap."

"Why can't I go to the conference?" whispered Tam as they passed the study.

"God preserve us from having the cast at a story conference. All you actors would get at the author to make their parts bigger. Anyway, your role's long enough."

"A hundred and seven lines, and a few more here and there would make all the difference," she said. Bernard smiled to himself, thinking how often actors discussed the quantity of their lines like misers counting sovereigns.

Down in the kitchen he explained to Harriet how sorry he was not to have let her know, but the conference had only been fixed half an hour ago. It was clear to Harriet that he took her seriously, and this touched her.

When his task of smoothing her was completed, he said:

"I wish we could persuade you to change your mind over what we were talking about last night. It means a lot to Sir."

"My mind's made up, Bernard," Harriet said, starting on a new loaf which she clasped under one arm like a baby.

When Bernard had left the kitchen, Tam asked:

"What was all that? What have I been missing?"

"Your father asked me to go to Italy with the unit," Harriet said, smiling faintly, so that the heavy lines down each cheek broke into angles.

"What a great idea, of course you must come! I need you!"

"You and your father can both save your breath," said Harriet, loosing Tam's throttling hug. "I am not tagging along as a camp follower to seventy people making a picture. I prefer my own kitchen and my own company."

"Pooh. Dad'll force you to come."

*

During the week before the unit left for Italy there were two or three preliminary rehearsals for the film. Most rehearsing would be on location before the actual shooting, but Clive Diamond and Robert Waring wanted to start work on the picture at once.

The Royalty's company of sixty-five actors provided a large part of the film cast; it took meticulous planning to release these actors, while the company still played at its London home and prepared for a regional tour.

Clive Diamond, the director of the film, had recently come back from Hollywood where he'd made one or two successful pictures but had been dissatisfied, because he found he had been given money instead of his own way. It was a fair exchange only if that was what you were willing to barter. Diamond needed to stop ingratiating the public; he considered his recent pictures had done this enough. Now, with America behind him for the time being, he and Waring had chosen the dangerous mixture of Shakespeare and a modern writer.

Diamond was forty, Jewish, on the fat side, rather bald, and with brandy-coloured eyes. He used his podgy hands like a man speaking Italian. His manner was wooing, he never raised his voice. Women adored him, and he was always with some beauty whom he would leave heartbroken when he moved on to the next. According to Robert Waring, he was a director that actors would follow over a cliff.

Tam had met him a dozen times at home, and was excited at the thought of working for him.

The first rehearsal was held in the Royalty's old rehearsal

37

room at the back of the theatre. This had been a boxers'
gymnasium, and leather horses and parallel bars remained,
used by the company for limbering up. When Tam arrived,
the first thing she saw across the room was David Bryden's
carrotty hair.

He saw her and came over.

She waited for him to mention that she was in the
picture, but he merely said :

"I didn't see you at the conference yesterday. I heard you
laughing in Bernard's office."

"I wasn't allowed to put my nose round the door."

"Pity. You missed some fireworks."

"Were you part of them?" asked Tam.

"No. It was the acting bit and not the screenplay bit.
Your father and Clive. Guess who won! By the way, I'm
coming to see *As You* to-night. I gather it's the last night."

She was glad to know he was coming to see the play :
actors always hear that particular news with added vivacity.
She said she hoped he'd like the production, adding that
Rosalind was gorgeous. Tam said this deliberately in case
he should imagine her guilty of the actress's usual opinion
that she could play a lead better than whoever was playing
it at present.

"I'll look forward to it," he said, and lounged off, looking,
with his vivid hair and rangy figure, like an actor himself.
Hadn't she once cast him as Orlando? Watching him go,
she thought that she liked him better.

The flight to Sicily was scheduled for the day following
the close of *As You Like It*. It was not a "last night" as
theatre people used to think of them. There would be no
end-of-the-production party, onstage speeches and offstage
nostalgia, and no flowers creaking in cellophane would be
presented to the leading actress, dewy with tears. The
Royalty was a permanent ensemble and when a play finished
nobody cried. They were rehearsing another.

At the end of the performance, Tam dumped her rustic
costume of Audrey into the corner of the dressing-room
for the last time, unhooked the stays that pushed her waist
in and bosom upward, and pulled off the long-tongued red
shoes. She swept everything off her dressing-table into a

large handbag, and kissed her room-mates. They were envious and well-wishing. "We're green with jealousy—send us a card—bring us back some Italian eyelashes, everybody says Sicilian hair's the thickest!"

Tam ran down the staircase, and on the way met a dozen members of the company. Some were still in costume, walking slowly in their heavy robes, with faces monstrously enlarged or altered by make-up. Some were already in street clothes. The older actors, many of them friends of her father's, said good-bye to her affectionately. But there were some edged good wishes from one or two of the young actors and actresses, who didn't conceal that they thought Tam was doing all right because she was "Sir's daughter."

Out in the square, she saw the Rolls parked in its usual corner, and when she went to the car, both her father and David were sitting together.

"You were both in front!" she exclaimed, pleased.

"I only saw the last act. David saw the whole performance. Hop in," said her father.

Tam climbed into the front of the car, half-waiting for a compliment from David. Compliments were part of the life of the theatre, a sort of token you passed to people, and they to you. These compliments, like the pieces of coloured plastic used in gambling, could have £500 or 5/- on them, but some token of high or low value was essential. And if you talked for twenty minutes about an actor's performance, he would still be sorry when you stopped.

All David muttered was:

"I really have to go. Haven't packed yet."

"Change your mind and have some dinner with us," said Robert Waring.

"All kinds of things to do . . . sorry."

David got out of the car, and with a hurried good night, walked away fast.

Tam stared after him.

As the car moved off she said:

"What was all that about? I don't think I like that young man much."

Her father was silent for a moment, and then said:

"Close the screen, Tamara."

The "screen" was a sliding glass partition that Robert Waring had found it necessary to have in his cars so that he could rehearse aloud. The first screen had been fixed after one driver had swerved straight into a ditch when his employer exclaimed savagely:

"I'll have your liver and your tripes!"

Tam pushed the screen shut, and turned to face her father. She had rehearsed the film all morning, had played two performances, and looked as fresh as somebody who has just had a bath and breakfast; energy and good spirits were like a scent around Tam.

He studied her for a while.

"Your Audrey's gone off a bit, hasn't it?"

Her face fell like a disappointed child's.

"I know Audrey's been history now for a quarter of an hour," he said. "But it's relevant for the future. Something in your recent playing . . . not at first . . . but lately, hasn't been right." He rubbed his chin. "Something's crept in."

She was listening as anxiously as a patient to a doctor's diagnosis, her eyes not moving from his face.

"The fact is, Tamara, that you may be a baby in some ways, but that performance of yours was hard."

He repeated the word: "Hard."

She swallowed.

"Do you think I am?" she said, at last, looking away.

He smiled slightly. His face softened.

"I know you aren't, puss. I know exactly how you are. That isn't our problem . . ."

"I can alter my playing."

"I hope so."

Something in his tone alarmed her.

"What is it? It's David Bryden! What's he said to you?"

"Rather a lot. He was at the performance this evening, as you know, and he telephoned me in the interval. He sounded upset. I drove down to watch the last act with him, and we've been talking. That's why he wouldn't stay and have dinner with us; he's just told me he would prefer you not to be in the picture."

40

2

Tam said:

"He doesn't *want* me?"

"He thinks you're too hard for the part."

"But it's *you* who makes the decisions——"

"No, no, Tamara, it's no good saying that since I want you to play in my picture, it doesn't matter a straw what the author thinks. Of course I can override him and of course that isn't the point. In the creative thing, as you know very well or should do, one cannot ride rough."

"You always ride rough."

"Do I?"

The mocking tone hurt her. What did her father mean? What did David Bryden mean? In what way was she hard? Was she hard-skinned, thick-skinned and so missed things? Was she wearing some kind of mental carapace that lessened the human understanding so vital to an actress?

The Rolls drove up the hill into the road edged with trees and stopped at the door of the house. A number of the windows were brightly lit, and at the look of a busy, occupied house, she shuddered.

"There's nobody at home, don't tremble like that. It's all right, all right, sweetheart," her father said soothingly. "Come along, I'll take you up."

"Dad is treating me as if I had the flu," she thought, as he put a heavy arm round her waist, and walked with her up the stairs to his study where, a few nights before, she had been so happy.

She went over to the fireplace and knelt on the rug, crouching like somebody with a pain in the stomach. Robert Waring poured her a glass of wine and walked over to give it to her. Tam put it on the floor without drinking it.

"You're not much of a fighter, are you?" he said suddenly.

"I don't know what you mean."

"I mean supposing every time a young actress didn't get a part she wanted she collapsed as if somebody had kicked her in the guts."

"That's how I feel."

"That's very obvious."

His tenderness was quite gone and Tam muttered:

"What's there left to fight for? I've lost."

"Indeed?" he said, "*You* may have done but I haven't. I'm a good fighter. The best I know. And if you think I intend to let that young man get rid of you—a Waring!— you still don't know much about me."

"But you said——"

"I said I don't ride rough-shod over people, actors, writers and so-on. Only damned fools do that. One has to box clever. I believe you'll make a good Miranda," he said, folding his arms and regarding the crouched figure, his head on one side. "You're still a bit of a child, as I've remarked before. You have a little shell of toughness, like most actors, or let's say I thought you had. The shell's necessary, or an actor would never take the knocks. Your trouble is that you're still new, and you let your protective shell show now and then. Bryden's young and given to instant decisions where his work is concerned. He's a very dedicated; sometimes he's a bit too religious about it for me and I wish he'd get down from the pulpit."

He walked about the room, drinking his wine between sentences, and unperturbed by his daughter's gloomy silence.

"Of course Bryden doesn't know the motion picture business and he still thinks the writer's the mainspring. He doesn't realise that once he's delivered the screenplay he isn't—not to put too fine a point on it—a very vital part of the picture. There are directors who work closely with their writers, cosset them. Clive isn't one of those. Bryden will just have to get used to it . . . Good! Here comes supper!"

Harriet had come in, followed by Ventura and Roberto, two of the Italian family who helped in the house, also

42

laden with trays. The Italians adored Robert Waring, and always waited on him with melting smiles, though later, in the kitchen, they fought Harriet and each other.

As Harriet was leaving, her brother put out an arm and caught her by the belt of her overall. When Ventura and Roberto had gone, he let her go.

"Coming to Italy with me?" he inquired.

Harriet did not answer, but glanced over at Tam huddled on the floor, and raised her eyebrows.

"I know, she looks like a shot partridge. It's very annoying."

"Who's been shooting her?"

"David Bryden. Asked me to take her out of the cast of *Tempest 72*. Doesn't want her."

"Doesn't he, by God," said Harriet, sitting down slowly.

"Well, well, that's what we're talking about, Harry," said her brother briskly.

"I suppose if she doesn't go to Italy she'd better stay comfortably at home with me," Harriet said.

Robert Waring had been cutting himself a slice of game pie. He swivelled sharply round to face her.

"Is that the direction of the wind?"

"Pretty much."

"You don't want to come?"

To Tam's strained attention, her father seemed far more moved by Harriet's news than by her own ruined future.

"No, dear, I don't want to come," said Harriet, folding her arms with a gesture not unlike Robert Waring's own. It was midnight, yet she was still wearing the white overall her brother had so often demanded that she should relinquish. The overall gave Harriet her independence and authority, and both of them knew it.

"But how can you not want to come when I *need* you, Harry?" he said with his mouth full. "We're going to make a lot of money out of this movie and though you're an unworldly old thing, it may possibly interest you to know that we hope to bring a lot into this country. The gnomes who want us to earn dollars will be pleased. When you come to Italy with the unit, you'll be working for England."

This call to patriotism left Harriet cold.

43

"Do you know exactly how many people are going to be running about after you while you're making this film?"

"Not exactly—" he said airily.

"Bernard counted them. There are seventeen."

"I make it nineteen. You'll be the twentieth. Excellent."

Harriet gave a snort of laughter, and Robert Waring laughed too. "So that's settled," he said.

She went over to take his plate, choose him some more food, fill his glass. He enjoyed being waited on by his sister, and stood passively.

"I know exactly what you're up to," she said. "And it won't wash. You have some boy scout idea that I need a holiday and this is your way of getting me to take one. You have decided to persuade me that I'm needed when all you really want is to see me sitting about in the sun outside a four star hotel. Darling——" She never used the word and so it was potent. "I know when you need me."

He put down his plate, came over and gave her a hug so tight that it took her breath away.

"I never heard such selfishness!" he said. "You're the worst of the lot—you want *nothing*. All right, stay behind if it makes you happy. You're damned spoiled. Always have been."

"And I'll stay behind too," said Tam drearily.

Robert Waring released Harriet and said impatiently:

"Get up, Tamara, get up. I'll thank you to stop looking like a dead bird in one of those Dutch still-lifes I've always disliked. Where's the character you're rumoured to have inherited from me? I don't see a sign of it. Cut a piece of pie."

*

The Caesario Hotel was built on a stony plateau half-way up a mountain facing the sea. In the 16th century it had been a nobleman's house, and the carved mailed fist holding a dagger still threatened, brave and forlorn, over the gateway. The open courtyard was filled with flowers and a fountain splashed in a marble basin with a mossy edge. The hotel itself was greyish-pinkish stone, pitted with age and weather. The hall was tiled, the broad staircase was curved and the stone walls were hung with fading tapestries. The huge bedrooms still kept an air of having once been slept in by Italian duchesses, and the ghosts of vanished pride and dead gallantry remained, but only to those who listened or concentrated.

Robert Waring, Clive Diamond and Tam were booked at the Caesario; the rest of the unit, the actors and crew, were at other hotels dotted over the small island. Everybody was reasonably satisfied with their accommodation . . . a rare state of things in film-making.

It was an hour since the plane had brought Tam and Bernard from London and they sauntered slowly down the road from the hotel towards the village. After the crisp autumn in London, the sun was burningly hot, the heat as heavy as if they were wearing it. Tam had changed into a blue shift and sandals. Her hair was damp from having just had a shower; it stuck to her forehead.

"Feeling more cheerful?" asked Bernard as they walked.

"Not till I know it's really on."

"Of course it is. What Sir says Sir does."

"Oh I know the part's mine," she said earnestly, "and I know Dad broke the news to David yesterday and I'm sure he was clever about the way he did it. But I feel odd just the same."

She peered at him for reassurance.

"I told you how it would be, Tamara," Bernard said, using the calm voice that worked with the actors with whom he spent his life, "Sir and Clive want you. Clive likes your work, and he'll also tell David he does, which will help a lot. Clive likes his actresses very young, it's one of his things that the young must be played by the young; Clive's as convinced as Sir is that you'll pull it off. The reason Sir and not Clive told David was because otherwise David might get it into his head that he'd offended Sir, as you're his daughter. Situations of that kind are to be avoided at all costs," added Bernard ponderously.

Switching the subject but still keeping to the film because it would interest her, Bernard told her that he had just seen Sara de Lullo's designs for some of the sets and costumes.

Sir had received them yesterday and was pleased with them.

"When's she coming to the island?" asked Tam.

"She was over before we came. For a couple of weeks. And she'll be around later. I know Sir thinks there's a lot to be got from being on the island . . . the sea and the rocks and ruins and so on," said Bernard, waving a hand at a commonplace villa with green shutters. "Of course she's coming. But she did tell your father that some of Baudelaire's best verse was about the East and he never went farther than Marseilles."

They slopped along the white road, a fine dust rising with their footsteps. Tam nervously concentrated on the coming film, avoiding the thought that she would soon have to face David Bryden, who had rejected her work and consequently had rejected her. She began to talk again. She asked Bernard why the film was to be made mainly with hand-held cameras. Didn't they normally move on dollies which made the action smoother?

"Clive doesn't want the film smooth at all. He is getting away from that with 72. Says he thinks the difference between a picture made with the hand-held cameras and one on a dolly is the difference between a live man and a corpse."

"Hand-held cameras jog all over the place," Tam said irritably. "A sequence I saw recently made me sea-sick."

Bernard said nothing.

She sighed and took his arm, squeezing it tightly. He gave hers a pressure in return. He knew she thought of him, treated him, as just an arm to hang on to. But she was holding his arm, and that was enough for Bernard.

The piazza in the village was rather sedate; it was Sunday. The cafés were closed, the children had all been to Mass and wore socks and best clothes, the boys with their hair slicked down and the girls in clean cotton dresses. Groups of people talking under the trees were also sedate : dark suits and respectable dark dresses, cardigans and silk scarves. Tam and Bernard, walking by in beach clothes, looked like rich gypsies.

Bernard had already spent a week on the island, and he

46

led the way through the narrow streets and out on to a road leading uphill towards the cliffs and the outline of a ruined Roman temple. It was actually this temple, with its pillars and hunks of broken carving, which had decided Clive and Robert Waring on the choice of the location.

The island, only an hour or so by boat from Sicily, was small and growing fashionable. But autumn was here, the beaches were no longer covered with parasols and sundecks, bars and pedalos; there was seaweed instead. The Roman relics on the island had never been particularly admired by archeologists, and had the advantage of being fairly unknown. Nobody as yet had filmed a murder there, or photographed for *Vogue*.

The temple was at the top of a cliff overlooking the sea, and the road winding up to it was steep. On either side, covered with flowering mosses and greyish lichens, were dry stone walls. Behind these were olive groves and fields full of thatched glass frames, in which the small-headed local carnations were grown. The air hummed with insects in the sunshine, and there was the far-off sound of a plane. As Tam walked along, she could smell thyme.

At the top of the road stood a cluster of umbrella pines, and beyond these was the ruined arch of the temple, grey stone against the deep blue sky.

Bernard glanced at Tam as they walked; she looked nervous, her face was pale above the vivid colour of her dress.

Short grassy downland grew round the ruins and a dozen cars belonging to the unit were parked under the pine trees. As Bernard and Tam came nearer they saw the actors, six or seven of them, sitting on fallen pillars and pieces of stone littered below the temple arch.

Robert Waring and Clive Diamond were talking to the production manager; the camera crew stood by patiently. Electric cables of different colours lay in thick coils all over the ground for yards around, and Tam and Bernard had to pick their way over them.

The actors, in jeans and T shirts, were silent in the bright sun : relaxed and thoughtful, content to sit and

47

wait. Diamond and Robert Waring moved over to talk to the lighting cameramen, a lanky man with a big nose called Rye Ingsoll, discussing where the camera would be set up, how the first shots were to be composed.

Clive saw Tam and came over to put his arm round her. He was stylishly dressed in cream coloured trousers and a fine apple green shirt; he always looked to Tam as if he'd just had a bath.

Still with his arm round her, he walked her away from the rest of the company.

"Lovely to see you. Sir told me about the trouble with David, which is all fixed now. You are not to worry, my darling."

The endearment, used by people in entertainment for a hundred years, was meaningless. It meant less than the use of her Christian name. Yet, spoken in Clive Diamond's cooing voice, Tam was glad to hear it.

"David's screenplay is fine. I'll even say it's brilliant, but casting the picture is my business. I saw your Audrey, darling, and she was *very* sexy!" He patted her on the bottom and walked away.

Tam sat down on a marble slab in the sun with the rest of the actors. She was relieved that there was no sign of David, and she settled down to wait and watch the setting up of the scene. This afternoon was to be spent in rehearsals.

Soon the assistant director called out :

"Quiet please, everybody. Rehearsal starting!"

The arc lights went up, one by one. It was curious to see them used in the bright sun, seemingly swallowed by it. Yet it was the lights which would pale the ink-black shadows thrown by sunlight, and the lights which could enhance or soften the images on the screen.

The rehearsal began with a scene from Shakespeare's *Tempest*, which was to be followed by one from the Bryden play. Miranda, with her father Prospero, meets her future lover, Ferdinand, for the first time. Ferdinand was played by Peter Moneto, a coltish young actor of twenty-two, already experienced in films.

Her father, in the leading role of Prospero, spoke his lines in a low voice, he was only walking through the part at present, and had not yet started to act it. Tam was immersed in her role as she stood beside him. She spoke Miranda's lines when she first sees Ferdinand :

"I might call him
A thing divine, for nothing natural
I ever saw so noble."

"Right!" called Clive, breaking into the scene with a chopping movement of his hand, a favourite gesture. "Okay for now. Thank you, ladies and gentlemen!"

Tam returned to real life as suddenly as if she'd fallen out of a window. Peter Moneto grinned and lit a cigarette. Her father strolled over to Clive. Tam glanced hazily round and found David Bryden staring straight at her.

It was the moment she'd been dreading. She looked away, hoping to see somebody she knew whom she could talk to, but the rest of the cast were already trailing to their cars, or setting off to walk towards the village. There was no sign of Bernard. It was like the end of a picnic, and only the camera crew, discussing to-morrow's scene, stayed in a group with Ingsoll. But they were moving away too, and she was alone.

She walked over to David.

He was leaning against the broken Roman arch and as she came across to him he didn't stir.

"I'd like to say something——" she began.

"Spare me the bit you rehearsed with Sir!"

The tone was so cutting that she took an involuntary step backwards.

"But didn't Dad explain——"

"He certainly did. He 'explained' very nicely. Brilliantly, one might say. He didn't hurt my feelings for a moment. But your father knows, and Diamond knows, and you know, too, don't you, that I didn't want you to play Miranda. Casting is not my job, of course. *They* are making the picture. I merely wrote the thing. What your father did not say, but is perfectly obvious, is that they intend to scrap a lot of my stuff anyway, and get in somebody else who'll do as he's told. I've been assured many times how lucky I am they are making the picture at all. Great. But I know the Miranda of 72 . . ."

While he'd been talking he hadn't once looked at her, but now he lifted his eyes and finished, ". . . and you're all wrong for her."

She stood still.

"I'll show you I can do it," she said. "But I don't have to talk to you, and I won't."

She spoke loudly, and ran down the path towards the village. It was only when she was home that she allowed herself to cry.

*

During the days of intensive rehearsing that followed, the scenes were set in the various sites that were to be used for the picture . . . a small beach, the temple, a cave by the shore, an olive grove on the cliff top. The actors had the usual difficulties of costume and make-up. Clive and Robert Waring had other troubles. Making a picture was complex and complicated, a curious mix of directing, acting, and the powerful presence of the camera. Always in close consultation they worked with the lighting cameraman at the composition of scenes; they studied shots in a finder and argued over camera angles. They stood about, talking as earnestly as leaders in a guerilla war.

The whole island knew about the film : the arrival of a unit of technicians, actors and crew, up to eighty people, was like the invasion of an alien race. Cars and vans hurried over the island bringing messages. Every hotel at which members of the unit were staying had telephones shrilling, night and day. Men with walkie-talkies could be seen in the village, or patrolling the olive groves, or striding along the beaches.

The Caesario hotel, which prided itself on a rich detachment, was unwillingly interested too. The barman talked about the film, and so did the one millionaire, a short-tempered man who usually concentrated only on the menu. The rich find other rich people of interest, and the Caesario

50

hotel's guests enjoyed hearing that one of the world's most famous actors rose at dawn, and worked as hard as a navvy.

It had been a particularly arduous day of rehearsals. The unit had worked since first light on some scenes on the beach; they hadn't stopped until the light faded. David had been around all the time, with Clive and Robert Waring. He had actually re-worked a scene on the set, scribbling in a book on his knee.

He avoided Tam, keeping as far away from her as possible.

Tam was aching with tiredness when she came down to dinner at nine o'clock. The dining-room, at the beginning of the "Dead Season" was almost empty. Here and there a table was occupied by a couple dining late in the hot evening : candles glowed on darkly tanned faces and diamonds. Most of the hotel guests were middle-aged or old. The summer people, all young, had gone.

Tam crossed the dining-room and went out on to the terrace where her father was sitting at a large tiled table in a corner by the glass wall. The table was bare except for a brandy glass filled with milk and a lighted candle. The wavering flame exaggerated his bony face.

"Why aren't you in bed asleep?" he said.

As she sat down she sighed.

"May I remind you that Miranda is fifteen-years-old and I don't want a clapped-out old stay-up who looks twenty-five. Your call is at six-thirty a.m. to-morrow morning."

A waiter appeared with a lighted candle, which he placed piously in front of Tam. As he handed her the menu her father took it away.

"You must have a quick meal. What do you fancy? Lobster?"

"Lovely."

"It will give you indigestion and probably a red nose. Medallion of chicken?"

"Gorgeous."

"They use garlic in the sauce. Suppose I wish to kiss you good night. Would you enjoy a juicy little steak?"

51

"Very much."

"Red meat overheats the blood."

"Stop playing Petruchio!" exclaimed Tam.

"What was that?"

"I said Petruchio. Harriet always said you're a natural-born tyrant. You know I'm tired and hungry so you automatically start keeping the food out of reach. If you could stop me eating at all, like poor starving Kate, you would."

"So I would if I thought it would get a performance out of you," he said, pleased with himself.

He called the waiter, ordered a meal in Italian (he enjoyed speaking Italian), and sipped his milk with relish. He was in a good mood.

He began to talk to her about his own ideas of the film, and Clive's, and how the two were knitting together. In the old days, the film producer had only represented the money, but all this was changed now, and that was why the idea of producing interested him. The producer was the man who made the film happen, got it off the ground by gathering into a unit the key people he wanted, artists and technicians as well as money men. The producer chose the director. Clive, said Robert Waring, was always original and sometimes brilliant. It was so good to have Clive.

They were working together at present on the comic scenes. Film jokes must be visual, preferably with hardly a word . . . like with the masters, Chaplin, Keaton, Tati. Tam, listening, nodded. She knew her father's passion for comic genius, his ever strong bent, as a great tragic actor, to be funny too.

"What do you think of Peter Moneto?" her father said.

"Fine."

"Bryden's enthused. Thinks the boy's the best young lead there is at present. I'm not sure he isn't right."

"Really?"

Her father looked at her.

"I suppose you wish he'd say it about you."

She usually rushed to justify herself and her work; she cared so much for his good opinion that it was absurd. But to-night she said nothing. She looked tired and rather beautiful, wearing a dress made of silver fringe which he had himself chosen for her. When she moved, the metallic stuff caught the candlelight and glittered.

"You can leave the rest of that sorbet," he said. "You're too tired to eat it. We must go. I to work, and you to bed. Do something for me, will you, Puss? I said I'd see Bernard in my suite. Pop up and wait for him for a moment or two. You know what a fusser he is, he'll start ringing round to find me. Tell him I'm with Clive and I'll see him on location at 8."

Tam walked with her father into the foyer. A car was waiting for him at the door. He was going to walk round the temple site at night with Clive, and to visit the beach; in the dark they'd still be working, sitting on pieces of masonry in the moonlight, smoking cigars and arguing while the patient driver sat in the car and waited, perhaps for hours.

"Good night, now. Kiss me," he said, bending down to Tamara. "Now don't stay chatting to Bernard. Just say to him——" he turned at the swing doors and spoke in quotation marks, " ' Dad says a short chat will do us both good but only for 10 minutes.' He'll get the point."

He went off, humming to himself.

Tam took her father's key and walked up the staircase. Tapestries hung on the walls in the subdued light, and from these, faces from the past looked down at her. Along the dim corridor were old faint mirrors framed in silver, and smoky oil-paintings. Faces peered from these too, as if through veils.

Her father's suite of rooms, a salon, bedroom and study facing the sea and opening on to a long balcony, were on the right of the passage. Tam unlocked the double doors and went into the salon, switching on a single light which burned dimly in an ugly glass shade. She walked out on to the balcony to smell the night-flowering lilies. In the distance she saw the long smooth line of the sea in the moonlight. It was still.

There was a quick step behind. She turned:

"Bernard, love——"

53

It was David Bryden.

The film had been rehearsed for days, but all through this time she and David had completely ignored each other: they hadn't exchanged a word.

"I have an appointment with Sir Robert," he said briefly.

"Oh—but he said——"

"What did he say?"

Tam exclaimed suddenly: "Damn my father!"

He did not bother to ask what she meant, but lit a cigarette and merely stood. She walked over to the sofa and sat down.

"Isn't it ridiculous," she said.

"I don't know what you mean," he replied coldly. "Your father said he wanted to talk to me, and told me to be here punctually at half past ten."

His face was closed and incurious. It occurred to Tam that he didn't trust her.

"He told *me* to wait for Bernard and explain that he's gone off to see Clive. He said 'tell him a chat will do you both good.' I suppose he thought it was funny to throw us together."

"Do you?" he said, without expression.

"No. No I don't. But perhaps he's right and we might talk for a minute."

She looked at him uncertainly, the silver dress sending out small dazzling rays.

"If you want to," he said.

He sat down on the other side of the room, below another wall hanging of Italian tapestry. It was a hunting scene, with crowds of figures riding through a forest. Just as the faces on the stairs had seemed to look down at Tam, so now the dusty embroidered faces studied David. They were pale with age and belonged to hundreds of years ago, all their sex and all their wars were gone. David, his hair like fire, was alive.

"Please make it easier. It's hard to talk about it again."

"Why try?"

"I want to. Will you give me a chance with Miranda?"

He didn't speak for a minute or two.

"How can what I say make any difference?"

Tam, practised at the variations of a voice, heard the slight change.

"It's what you think that I mind about," she said. "I know Clive gave me the part, but *you* know I'm Sir's daughter. I hate using who I am. I never want to, believe me, it's true. I want to be myself, not be slotted into a movie of my father's as his little pet. Do you believe me?"

"I suppose so."

Suddenly it seemed desperately important to explain herself to him, not to please or flatter him but to speak plain truth.

"I never told you why I was so greedy about getting the part," she said. "You think I'm just an actress mad for it because it is opposite Sir and in an important picture. That's true. Of course it's true. But I wanted to play in *Tempest 72* for so many other reasons . . . because it's beautiful and your words always have a strong effect on me. They're so sad and harsh and funny. They go to the heart."

Almost before she had finished speaking, David came across the room towards her. He put his arms round her, and gave her a hard, passionate kiss.

*

"The signorina has a half-hour only."

The maid pulled the curtains, and the heavy curtain rings jangled together. She put a tray of coffee beside the bed; Tam woke slowly, propping herself on her pillows. The sky outside the window was still black.

She poured the coffee unsteadily, stupid with sleep, and then, with a sudden shock, almost a stab of pain, she remembered David. She thought of his cold manner, his unrelenting face, and the sudden, violent kiss. If only one could recreate kisses; lock them up in a desk or put them on a record, so that they could be played over again. She thought of kissing him and she thought : "I know so little about him still." It was exciting that discovery was yet to come.

But did a kiss, given only because she'd moved him by talking about his work, mean she had the right to walk in and out of his life as if it were a house open to the public? She enjoyed revealing herself to her friends. Perhaps he would resist this. Her father had once told her that she judged what others would do by her own reactions and that it was absurd. "People are as different as the patterns on the palms of the hands," he had said. "Thank God for it. It gives actors something to work on. Observe them. Love them if you can manage it. But don't try and solve them, as if they were mottoes in a cracker."

She dressed in a thick white sweater and slacks, and hurried down the stairs. Bernard was in the hall, looking at his watch.

"They've gone. We're the last. No, don't bother to tell me why you're late. Just come on!"

They climbed into a brake, one of those hired for the unit and which darted like mosquitoes all over the island. They drove fast along empty dark roads.

Dawn was breaking, the sky dim and clear of cloud. The leaves on the vines were withered and the grapes were picked.

Bernard put his hand over Tam's.

"Your big scene to-day."

"*One* of my big scenes!"

"Your scenes with Sir are the ones I call scenes."

"You and Sir. When's it going to wear off? By the way, he gave me a message for you last night. He said he'd see you on location before eight."

"That was a joke. We had breakfast at half past five and the croissants choked me. He's started his autobiog again."

Tam groaned in sympathy. It had been her father's habit for the last few months to dictate bits of his life and thoughts into a tape recorder; it would, he said airily, make at least three books. Bernard had been rash enough to suggest that Robert Waring might prefer dictating to him. The offer was accepted promptly—the tape machine bored him and he liked Bernard's company. So now, late or early, Bernard would be dragged away to take down: "When I saw Giovanni he talked for some time about Pirandello. Giovanni is old and dry. That's good, isn't it, Bernard? I re-

56

member his hands were like waxed paper. Where are we?"

Tam said she had gathered that they were stuck on the autobiography because of some libellous bits.

"That's his alibi when he doesn't want to get on with it. Libel doesn't slow your father down, Tamara : some of the chapters we haven't yet pruned would cost thousands in damages."

Bernard turned the car by a small grey church, its spire topped by a black statue of a madonna. The shape, its arms stretched to the dawn, was menacing rather than benevolent.

"There we are," said Bernard, nodding towards a path overlooking a beach. Vans and lorries were parked, and actors were already standing around in costume. The untidy haphazard gathering might have been people clustered together on a badly-organised protest march; in the sad morning light they looked cold and tired. Some of the actors had blankets wrapped round their shoulders over their costumes, others were drinking coffee. The production manager wore a tweed cap, the flaps down over his ears. One of the camera crew had tucked both hands, for warmth, under his arms.

The sun began to shine faintly down on the reddish beach where Robert Waring and Clive Diamond, seated at a bamboo table, resembled generals on the dawn of a battle. The papers spread in front of them could have been war-maps.

Waring was doing the talking. He had spent hours last night on the script and was explaining his proposed changes, point by point. He was quite aware that even the smallest alteration would throw the shooting; that the plans already made were complex and delicate, interlocking like the pieces of a watch. But he was an actor and the mechanics of filming—cameras and choice of lenses, angles and spun glass filters, close-ups, long shots and fades, were so many aids to his art. And these aids could be pushed around if he wanted to push them.

"The scene wouldn't have worked as it was before," he finished. What he meant was : "The scene would have petered out when I left it, so I've written myself back in."

"I thought we agreed that it would be good if Miranda was alone for a moment or two," remarked Clive, slowly

57

fixing the script open on the table with two pebbles from the beach.

"Yes, but it's more interesting now. You see."

Clive knew what Waring was doing, and the star knew that he knew. Two conversations were going on at the same time. It was like a drink that has cream on the top and brandy underneath : if you were experienced, you knew how to get to the brandy right away.

Tam, unaware that her father was shaving down her screen time, came down on to the beach with Bernard beside her.

"Good morning Clive. Hallo, Dad. Are we starting soon? I've got butterflies."

"You don't need quite so many butterflies after all, darling. The script has been altered just a fraction . . ." murmured Clive dryly, but went on to explain the changes persuasively. Waring nodded, murmuring, "That's good. That's better. Clive's the smart one around here."

Tam took the news that part of her scene had been cut as coolly as she could; she was not in a position to argue.

Before the rehearsal started her father said, "By the way. How was your pal the author last night?"

"Dad! What a trick to play on me!"

"But naturally it worked."

*

Two of the vans used by the unit, large circus-style vans, were travelling dressing-rooms. Tam went over when the rehearsal finished to change into costume and make-up.

Preparation in the theatre before a performance was a leisurely routine that she always enjoyed, her costumes would be hanging neatly in the corner of the dressing-room and if there were changes during the play the clothes would be hung in sequence. There was also someone in Wigs or the Wardrobe at hand if there were difficulties. And there was as much time as you wanted to dress, to make-up, and to prepare for the coming performance. It wasn't like this now. There was a team of three in the van, two girls—for make-up and costume—and a man who was responsible for dressing her hair. The make-up girl placed

58

Tam in front of a glass and started work on her face at once. The old days of heavy "slap" make-up to withstand the glare of blazing lights were in the past; film make-up now was more subtle, with eyes and brows, cheekbones or jawlines, delicately enhanced for close camera-work. And the effect was even lower key than that used for ordinary photography. The make-up girl at first did not seem to be doing very much. But as Tam watched, her own face vanished in the glass, and Miranda slowly appeared and stared at her. As she saw the materialising face of the character she was to play, she used her fancy so that the Miranda who had taken possession of her physical self could also take hold of her spirit.

Her only costume for to-day was a white bathing suit, fussed over by the girl in charge of costumes. Her only alteration in hairstyle was that the hairdresser streaked her hair with gold.

When all three of them had finished, they stepped back and looked at her observantly. She thanked them, and picked up a thin silk wrap. It floated away behind her as she walked from the van.

The sun was getting stronger, the sea sparkled, the waves were small; a fishing boat went by. On a rock at the edge of the shore was David, a battered script sticking out of his jeans pocket.

"There you are," he said.

She walked over and stood passively.

"You look lovely," he said. "Will you have supper with me to-night? We'll fix it later. Just say yes."

"Yes. Yes, of course."

They spoke quietly as if in the presence of some invisible being: the barrier that separated Miranda and Tam.

The arc lights began to go up one by one, feeble in the strong morning sunlight.

Clive called:

"Right everybody! Be prepared for irritating stops now and again. Bobbie: do you think a little more to the left?"

Tam took her place beside her father, who was standing in silence, withdrawn and relaxed. The actor playing Ariel was nearby, his body sprayed with green paint, his face fantastic with white and green. He was naked except for a piece of seaweed on a G string.

The clapper-boy held his slate in front of the camera.

"Slate 30. Take One. Track One."

There was the snap of the clapper.

The camera operator, a heavy camera strapped to his chest on a leather harness, was kneeling. The lights, covered with glass filters, shone in a ring. The technicians stood in a semi-circle, like people at prayer, absolutely quiet.

It was one of Tam's difficult scenes in the modern sequence. Prospero scolded her. And Miranda, crying out:

"Oh father—I can't do it——" had to run down the beach into the sea.

She did the run, barefoot across the sharp pebbles, the fall into the sea, and a few strokes. She did it twelve times. Each time, when the take was completed, Tam was hurried away to change into a fresh bathing costume, twenty of which, all identical, were in the van. Each time her hair was redone and her make-up fixed. Between takes she shivered, sipping endless coffees.

She was only dimly conscious that she was cold, was unaware of the sharp stones as she ran into the water. She faintly noticed that everybody else, from her father to the clapper-boy, was warm and dry.

Once again she ran into the sea.

"Good. That was good," Clive said. He was like a conductor, bringing up, or softening down a particular instrument. "Now this time I want you to do it slightly differently. As you run towards the sea you stumble. Shall we try it like that?"

When he talked, he wooed her. He himself gave a performance, showing the effect he wanted, clasping his hands, looking entreatingly towards Prospero. "Like this. And this. Okay?"

Tam stood and watched and nodded and shivered.

Now and again Clive peered through the huge viewfinder, like an astronomer examining the moon. Filming was a long way from the world of the theatre. *There* a player could move into Imperial Rome and command both legions and slaves for three hours at a time. There . . . often on a great stage filled with other actors . . . the world created by his imagination was shared by his fellows and by a willingly bewitched audience. But here in film-making the imagined world was a few feet square, surrounded by cables like a hundred snakes, and groups of figures in overalls. It was like acting among a gang of people setting up a coconut shy.

But when the voice cried :

"Slate 30. Take 10," the thing still happened. When Robert Waring spoke the same few lines, he turned at once from man to magician. Tam watched him make it work every time as beautifully and as perfectly.

"You must obey me !"

The words rang out, over and over, never damaged by repetition. They seemed to get brighter, as if by using, he polished them.

The break came for lunch at last. Tam, wrapped in a pink towelling robe, found she was tired and hungry.

She went with Bernard over to the canteen, her robe sticking to her damp back. Now that the performance was over for the time being, she returned slowly to her real self. Bernard murmured encouragements, sat her down under a tree and went to get her some lunch.

Looking up, she saw David.

He sat on the grass beside her.

"You must be exhausted."

"A bit damp. Was it all right?"

"Lovely. Lovely." There was a pause. "I must have been out of my mind," he added, so quietly that she could scarcely hear. "Forgive me."

She said nothing, but touched his arm. He said :

"May I pick you up at eight at the hotel? I have to go now. Clive wants something done to the script this afternoon. Tam."

"Yes?"

"You will come, won't you?"

"Of course."

61

He stood up, and unwillingly walked away.

Tam stayed hunched in the robe, moving her bare feet into a patch of sunlight.

Bernard returned with trays, and sat down beside her. "I was given Vichy for you. I'm told you are not allowed a glass of Chianti like the rest of us. And I don't need to say whose dictum that was!"

A woman's voice suddenly shouted:

"Hi, Bernie! Surprise, surprise!"

Looking up, Tam and Bernard found a woman standing beside them. She was thin and angular, with dangling earrings and a determined smile. She had picked her way through the crowds picnicking round the van, and sat down by Bernard, saying, "Glad to see your old pal?"

"Maggie! What brings you to Italy," exclaimed Bernard. "Do you know Tamara Waring?"

"Of course I do. I've worked with you at the Royalty, haven't I, Tam?" Maggie gave a hearty laugh, screwing her face into a grimace as if blowing a horn. She straightened her face out. "I'm on vacation; I heard Sir was here with you all, so I couldn't resist coming to have a sniff round. You can't keep me away from show biz, you know!"

Bernard went to get her some lunch, leaving his own to get cold. Maggie called "Oh no, really," and lit a cigarette. She stayed chatting with Tam.

Tam was rather dismayed at the new arrival. Maggie was one of those middle-aged women who flourish on the fringe of theatre or films, a fan who made her living by it. She'd worked in a photographer's, as an A.S.M., as a secretary in a TV company, had acted in rep, had even been a dresser. She was expert at touring abroad, or as an assistant floor manager on TV. She spoke film language, theatre shop, newspaper argot. Tam who knew her slightly and was uneasy about her, found Maggie hearty, energetic and kindly; a bit neurotic. Tam also thought her effusive and believed her affectionate manner to be false.

Now she talked about *Tempest 72*, apparently more up-to-date on the matter than Tam was.

"You saw it at the Court? But did you see the experimental version they did at lunchtime at the Arts? Milo directed. It was *brilliant*. My dear girl, how can you possibly make the picture if you didn't see Milo's production!"

"I daresay we'll manage," Tam said.

Maggie lit another Gauloise and inhaled deeply. Bernard arrived with food.

"My dear old mate, you shouldn't have bothered. What is it? Chicken pilaff. I never eat chicken when I'm in Italy. You never know with poultry, do you?"

After a while she wandered off "to say hallo to Sir," threading her way among the crew, all of whom she knew by names and nicknames.

"Sir is not going to be overjoyed at that," observed Bernard. "I can see myself having to remove her."

"She's a sticker," agreed Tam.

They sat for a while among the crowds, drinking their coffee in the shade from the thin-branched olive trees.

Breaks for meals were timed to the minute, for time literally *was* money in a movie, a day representing thousands of pounds. Everybody went back to their places, and rehearsals started for the next shots.

Tam, waiting for her cue, saw Maggie hobnobbing with one of the electricians.

Her father and she rehearsed a line together, and as they moved out of shot, Tam murmured:

"Maggie Street's arrived."

"I've just seen the old war horse," said her father. "Nice to have her around."

Tam's hope of her father having Maggie removed was not to succeed. It looked as if she was going to be grimacing around for some time.

When Bernard joined Tam before shooting started, she said in a low voice:

"Dad wasn't unwelcoming at all. He actually seemed pleased. I didn't know he even liked her."

"We forgot what a mad fan she is," Bernard said. "She rushed up to him with such outrageous compliments that Clive reeled."

"I suppose Dad licked his chops."

63

"Right. What's more he's asked her up to the hotel for a drink. We'll have to grin and bear it."

*

Filming went on until the shadows were too long to do any more. Clive was pleased. They had been working for ten hours, and had put three minutes in the can: that was a large amount of work to accomplish in a day. Three minutes. The time it took to boil an egg.

Tam was tired. Her skin was leathery from being all morning in the sea, and she was grateful to change into her thick sweater. She remembered she was having dinner with David to-night. At present she was too exhausted to react, and was glad to slump into the car with Bernard and drive back to the hotel.

"We're not going to find Maggie Street here, are we?" she said, as they drew up outside the Caesario.

"We might. I think you'd better go in the side door."

"Then *you'll* get stuck with her," said Tam, grateful and guilty.

"I'll be around until she runs out of compliments and the boss indicates that he wants me to get rid of her."

Tam went through the side door, exchanged smiles with a chambermaid who was film-struck, and went up to her room. Her legs were trembling. She fell into bed and five minutes later was deeply asleep.

She woke, dimly conscious of the sound of thunder. There it was again, louder. It was a series of thundering knocks on her bedroom door. The room was in darkness, and when she groped about and switched on the bedside light, she saw that it was after nine o'clock.

The knocks were repeated, and a voice called "Tam!"

She stumbled out of bed, and opened the door, blinking like an owl.

David was standing in the doorway, changed into a dinner jacket, and looking fresh and smart. When he saw her, he laughed.

"I thought I'd never wake you or that somebody had stolen you away! You haven't changed your mind, have you?"

"I'm sorry—I've been asleep——"

64

"I know. I feel so guilty waking you when you've had such a tough day. But do come. Will you? Just put on any old thing."

Tam put up her hand to her hair, in spikes from lacquer and sea water. She knew she looked squashed and dishevelled.

"What does it matter how you look when you're beautiful?" he said matter-of-factly.

"I'll be ten minutes. No more, I promise," she said.

When he had gone she peeled off her clothes, had a shower, and put on a long pink dress with a high waist, a dress that might have been worn in Napoleon's time. She clipped on earrings the colour of the dress, put on backless sandals, and ran down the stairs. He was sitting on the bottom step, to the disapproval of the assistant manager at the Reception desk.

"I like a lass who runs. Come on, we'll have to go through the garden. Sir's in the bar with a female who must be a gym mistress."

They crept through a salon into the dark and climbed into David's car, parked in the lane.

Tam suddenly felt quite unbearably happy. She was happy to be with David, whom she scarcely knew, yet whose words she spoke every day, words which sometimes made her cry. She was happy to be with David whose lively creased face pleased her. She was happy to be on the island; it was like Prospero's.

The moonlight washed the landscape. It was warmer to-night.

"Here's where I'm taking you," he said. "To some friends of mine who have cooked a meal for us. You'll like them."

He slowed the car outside a house which was too old and humble to be a villa. It stood back from the road in a patch of land edged with a crumbling, flower-starred stone wall. There was a little olive grove, a garden full of herbs, and a goat tied with a string to a post. It stood in the moonlight like a ghost.

David walked with Tam through the garden to the house; the door was ajar.

"This is where I'm lodging. I've known the place for ages. I wanted to surprise you."

"At last, at last!" exclaimed an Italian voice. A small woman with crinkly black hair came out to welcome them. She smiled as Italians do, raying it at Tam as if she were the only person in the world she wanted to see.

She took them into a room crowded with furniture, pictures, ornaments, mats, settees and vases of dried flowers. David introduced her. This was his friend Signora Gourielli, his great friend, and this . . . a fat figure emerged from the kitchen . . . was Signor Gourielli whose uncle had worked at the Savoy Hotel in London.

The Signor indicated that he could not speak English, and that he could not shake hands as his were covered in flour. He was, explained David, the village pastry-cook. The Signor bowed, beamed some Italian smiles of his own, and retired.

"Sit down, please to sit," said the Signora, drawing a chair for Tam. Supper would be ready in a moment, could she leave them while she dished it up. It was delightful to see the signorina! She bustled off, full of awe-inspiring goodwill.

The meal which followed, and which Tam and David ate alone in the over-furnished room, was delicious. There were stuffed vine leaves and aubergines, there were peaches spiced with ginger. The salad was made of marigold leaves, and one dish turned out to be fried marrow flowers.

"We have good wine but David says you are an artist and may not drink," said Signora Gourielli, reverently arriving with fruit juice as if serving Mass. She brought coffee, and went to find her husband in the kitchen. He was busy making batches of apple pies and cheese tarts for to-morrow. David and Tam complimented him on the supper, which had been superb.

The Gouriellis lingered for a while, in a cloud of smiles and compliments, and then rather regretfully bade the young people good night, explaining that both of them had to rise very early in the morning.

"Please don't hurry away. Stay and have your coffee and

perhaps one little liqueur," said Madame. "And David must show you the terrace. You will like the terrace."

Tam thanked her, and Signora Gourielli clasped her hands and said warmly that she must come again, many many times.

Tam and David were silent after the Gouriellis had gone upstairs, the stairs creaking loudly as the couple ascended. David took Tam over to a little settee; coffee was laid on a table nearby.

"What a lovely meal. What sweet people," she said.

"A bit overwhelming, all the benevolence, but you have to wade straight through it. Basically they're nice in spite of all that."

"I rather like them because of it."

He looked amused.

"That's because you're from the south, London. From Birmingham upwards we prefer a bit less charm and a bit more reality. But they're nice. I love them."

"How did you meet them? I never knew you'd been to the island before, unless you came here to look for a location?"

He laughed.

"No, it was nothing like that. As a matter of fact, it was the island that made me write the play. I wrote it in this room. Over there at that table with the daisy painted on it."

"In this room!" repeated Tam, gazing at the table in astonishment.

"Yes. If it hadn't been for the Gouriellis there wouldn't have been a *Tempest 72* at all. It was the winter before last; I'd been ill and I was feeling low and I borrowed the fare to come right down Sicily by train. It took for ever, but it was cheap. I slept in the train with my feet up. A man I knew at University, a real mate, wrote to the Gouriellis whom he's known for years, and said I wanted a week or two of change and some winter sunshine. Down I came. It poured with rain day and night. The Gouriellis were wonderful. They wouldn't let me pay them a penny. They fed me, taught me Italian, introduced me round the village. Then I started to write . . ."

"And that made you happy?"

He was leaning against the settee in a favourite attitude, as she'd first seen him on the plane to Paris, legs stretched out in front of him, studying his shoes.

"Writing isn't like that. It's a chore. A bore. Gives you backache."

"But you wrote a *masterpiece*!"

At the tone of her voice, he leaned towards her and took her face in his hands and gave her a rain of kisses, punctuating each with words.

"How did I dare——" kiss—"to say you were"—kiss—"hard?"

"Perhaps I am."

"You are lovely," he said. "Lovely. A beautiful actress. And a darling."

He pulled her to her feet.

"Now I have to show you Ma Gourielli's terrace. She'll never forgive me if you don't see it. Come along, glorious creature."

"Is there something special about it?" Tam asked. He linked her arm through his.

"Cactuses!"

The cicadas buzzed loudly in the dark as they tiptoed across a stony terrace, nearly falling over a loose stone. In front of them was a mass of flowerpots arranged on ledges.

"She's built a sort of cactus altar," said David. "The one she likes best is that long spiny devil. Like a demented sausage."

"It's very large!"

"It's very horrible. She says it flowers every ten years."

"It's too long to wait."

They began to giggle. Everything seemed funny: the cactuses with their uncomfortable prickly shapes, grotesque in the moonlight; the terrace, so stony that when they moved it was like walking on a shingly beach.

"Once I watered the big one and she said its personality was changed."

They didn't dare laugh aloud and Tam had to put her handkerchief in her mouth, something she hadn't done since she was at school.

David said :

"Now, stop. We must stop. I have to take you home, it's late."

But instead of walking to the house, he put his arms round her and pulled her close, looking down at her in the deceiving light. He kissed her.

Tam kissed him back, shutting her eyes. It was going right . . . all going right.

What did she want to say? Something? Nothing? He whispered in her ear :

"Your father's waiting. I can feel him sending out beams like radar."

They stayed and clung.

At last they pulled apart and went through the Gourielli house and out to the car. David switched on the dashboard light, saw the time on the clock and said, using her father's intonation : "Gentle heaven!"

Tam's feelings, blissful, turned to alarm as the car drew near the hotel which was still bright with lights. It was well after midnight and she imagined her father angrily waiting for her in the hotel foyer. It was the kind of thing he did.

"You'll have to go the back way again," David said, apparently thinking the same. The lane which ran down the side of the hotel was narrow, and as they coasted down the slope, flowering shrubs brushed the windscreen. He stopped the car under the hanging branches of a tree.

"Thank God there's a back way," she said. "I can just imagine Dad, like Destiny, standing there pointing a bony finger at me! I'd die of fright!"

As if the sight of her laughing face moved him he suddenly gripped her and bent forward and kissed her hard. When she put her arms round him, he gently loosed them.

"You must go. You need sleep, lovely girl. And to be fresh for to-morrow. We must say good night."

"Good night. Darling David."

He took her hands and leaned down so that his head was in her lap, and the dark drained the colour from his red hair. He looked up.

"We'll have lots of good times."

69

"Lots."

"But don't——"

"Don't what?" she echoed.

"Don't think me better than I am. You don't know me."

"I know your work."

"That's true. Yes. It's true. But it's only a part of me. The best part. You must promise me something."

"I'll promise you anything you like."

Stirred by him, she was not her quick observant self and missed the tone of his voice.

"Promise me you won't love me. Never love me, Tam."

She laughed and said good night. She ran through the garden feeling cold.

3

On some days during the shooting Tam was not called, and spent all day swimming and sunbathing. At other times, made up and in costume, she would have to wait at the place the film was set up that day, in case they wanted her even for a minute; the day would go by from dawn until dusk and she would not be used once.

Filming needed patience. It was so different from the stimulus and action of the theatre that Tam had to learn it, like a lesson. She had to learn to sit passive for hours at a time.

The morning following her supper with David, she was not called for the shooting until midday. She went down late to breakfast on the terrace.

It was a perfect day, clear and glistening, the kind of day that makes Italy to English eyes seem like the garden of Eden. From the black-and-white marble terrace she looked down a flight of steps into a garden full of flowers and shrubs. The grass glinted from a sprinkler whirling in a spray of water, the old wall, on the other side of which she and David had lingered last night, was covered with flowers.

When the waiter brought breakfast, she drank some of the coffee but found she couldn't eat. She was annoyed with herself for moping; it was ludicrous.

Tam was not used to brooding about anybody. The only thing that had ever filled her mind with worry or uncertainty had always been work—work alone had gripped her imagination until now.

She turned over in her mind what had happened last night. It had been extraordinarily happy and when she thought of how she'd felt, it had been light. Yes, light. As if at one time both she and David could have gone straight off the ground into the air.

She thought about kissing him; it had been sexy and beautiful. And over. What could she do now? The answer to that was simple—nothing. He'd wanted to be with her last night, and wanted her too, and just when she'd felt most intensely and had been most excited, he'd flattened it with the humiliating words: "don't love me."

Her coffee grew cold. The waiter asked, could he bring her some more? When he spoke, she gave a start. He was young, and he smiled shyly at her. "Coffee helps the concentration," he said, touching his forehead to indicate her fancy at work. He had the devoted look of a member of the audience, as if to say: "You are an actress, and therefore working to please me. What task can I perform to serve you in return? Name it!"

Tam thanked him and forgot to drink the coffee again.

She had always had plenty of masculine company and never needed to look for it. Men fell in love with her quite often; there were others who were in love, as her father pointed out, with "juicy parts in my theatre." But David had been neither of these things, and even now she was not sure how little or how much last night was going to mean. Her father often scoffed at the female habit of believing, too easily, that a man was caught. "One evening out and she thinks he's hooked," he would say. "It's pathetic. No woman's got a man just because he wants her in bed. Quite the contrary. Men want a woman. Then they don't want her."

"Oh Dad!" Tam had said impatiently. Confident of an effortless success with most men, and in love with nobody, she thought the conversation rather absurd. "Who's hooking anybody? Men are so conceited."

"You'll see. Women still believe a few kisses means a down payment on a house. It's astonishing how they don't change. I'll give you a good example. Theodosia."

He always gave his instances from plays or films. Theodosia had been a character in a recent play at the Royalty. Tam was unwise enough to protest: "But Dad, Theodosia wasn't real!"

"What's more real than a woman in the drama?" he'd demanded. "You'd better get your priorities right, my girl."

She left the hotel and walked towards the village, wishing she was needed on location now and didn't have to wait until noon. The white road was dazzling in the brilliant sun, there were flowers in the dry grass at the verge of the road, thick-stalked pink umbrella shapes, and lanky scabious the colour of dead lavender. In the distance a cluster of olives stood round an old tiled house. She went past a flat granite rock by the roadside; a lizard was sitting on it, its tail curved, its hands like little fans.

Down the road, Tam saw a familiar, angular figure striding towards her. A voice shouted: "Hi!"

It was Maggie Street. The older woman came up, walking as briskly as on a winter's day in England, exclaiming cheerfully that Tam was just the person she wanted: Bernard had told her Tam wasn't filming this morning, so why didn't they have a Campari and a gossip in the piazza.

"You can catch me up on the picture. It all sounds exciting, doesn't it? Of course I would find it exciting, as Sir's in it!"

Maggie rattled on, falling into step with Tam. "You know I've always been crazy about that father of yours. I was his A.S.M. before he started the subsidised theatre lark." She did not wear sunglasses, and screwed up her eyes as she talked. Her black bead earrings swung. Tam, murmuring polite replies, thought that it was Maggie's good humour and thick skin, energy and enjoyment of work, that managed to get her in everywhere. Evidently Maggie had dined with her father last night: *that* was the most difficult prize of the lot.

"I drank a lot of excellent brandy last night," said Maggie reflectively. "Though I must say your father didn't join me much. He says he isn't drinking. Since when?" "He never did."

"Most actors drink a bit, bless them. Why shouldn't they? And talking of drink, where's a bar?"

Women in the piazza were buying anchovies from wooden tubs, and spiny pink fish heaped on fig leaves. The children hopped in the dust. The largest of the three cafés had opened its umbrellas, and as Tam looked across, her heart suddenly jumped. Sitting under an umbrella, reading a paper, was David. She felt a sweep of pleasure and tenderness as she hurried over.

"Hallo," she said, bending slightly down.

"Hallo, Tam. May I buy you a drink?"

"Why not two? Remember me, your old friend Maggie? We met in Edinburgh last summer. I've been hearing all about the picture. It looks as if you've got a winner, I must say."

David bought drinks and Maggie drew up a chair, leaned on her elbows and talked. She was enjoying herself. Now and again, with elephantine tact, she attempted to include Tam in the conversation but it was obvious that the person she wanted to impress was David. She asked technical questions with great interest, and she listened to his replies, lighting a Gauloise, and breaking a match stick in half. She asked what Clive was like to work with? How did he and Sir hit it off? Was Rye Ingsoll as tiresome as people said?

David answered good-humouredly, and then with growing interest, as the conversation was exclusively his own shop.

Tam sat wishing Maggie Street—bead earrings, beady eyes and all—in the farthest TV studios in the coldest part of the British Isles.

73

Finally, Maggie said she must make a telephone call. "See you both on set!" she cried, saluting them; she had already made herself an established member of the unit.

It was time for Tam to go up to the temple where the film was being shot to-day: she and David walked along the road together.

"You don't like Madame Street much, do you?" he said.

"Do you?"

"A bit skittish. Useful, I daresay. She adores your father."

"So do a hundred million other people."

"But we don't have to buy them drinks. Never mind. Not to worry."

It was the identical voice, soothing, kindly, without a single overtone, that Bernard used to her.

*

In the weeks that followed, she saw David every day. They got on well together, and being involved in the same creative work, had a lot in common. Tam accepted his company with a bright face, and always hoped it would alter back to the way it had been the night they dined together. It didn't.

Four pairs of eyes watched them: Bernard was quiet; Clive Diamond was pleased; Maggie Street, still around, discussed them; Robert Waring said nothing. To Tam, her father's composed silence was depressing: he was normally so sharp about her friends. "That bad actor is wasting your time." "Where did you dig *him* up?" It was usually necessary to use diplomacy before her father would accept the presence of any man who liked her; he was inclined to label such admirers "followers." But now he made no comment, even when Maggie Street, drinking her way through the Campari bottle, cried: "That boy friend of yours adores you. It's quite touching!"

Robert Waring's attitude could mean only one thing: his intuition told him there was nothing between David and Tam. He was right. Tam couldn't fault David's manner to her, it was friendly, admiring, helpful, humorous. He never asked her out at night, but he was always around during the hours of shooting, always glad to encourage and talk to her: "You look gorgeous." "What do you think about slightly altering that exit line? I believe I could improve it."

When she arrived in the dawn with Bernard, wherever the film that day was set, David would already be there with Clive and her father. When the shadows, every day falling earlier and longer, stopped work, David was still around. He took her for walks across the island, to swim in rocky pools, to local movies of startling badness, with Bernard to make the third. The Gouriellis told him about two ponies, and once or twice in the morning when Tam wasn't needed they went riding on the long beaches in the scarcely-wrinkled sand. Tam always had dinner with her father and Clive at the Caesario at night, after both men had watched the day's rushes. These were shown on a small-screen projector in Robert Waring's private salon. Nobody else was present at the screenings except Rye and Bernard.

During dinner, after seeing the rushes, Clive and Robert never discussed them in front of Tam, though the conversation was always about the picture.

David often joined them at dinner, as Bernard did, and the table on the terrace was animated, the talk spirited. The candles, burning steadily in the windless night, would light four men and a girl: Robert Waring's famous face, bony and beautiful; Clive, fattish, at times rather prissy, reminding Tam of a man in Imperial Rome who enjoyed good living; Bernard, who listened more often than he talked; and David, with his brilliant hair and explosive entries into the talk, usually ready to disagree with the star. Turning from one to the other, sometimes the centre of their indulgent attention, Tam should have been happy.

But she was not. And when she was alone after some evening—or a whole day—spent in David's company, she sometimes thought of an incident that had happened at Glyndebourne.

It had been summer, and her father had driven her down to Sussex where he was meeting one of the directors. The weather had been sunny and warm, and her father had left her listening to a rehearsal while he went to his meeting.

75

The orchestra was tuning up before an overture, and Tam was taken in quietly and given a chair in the corner of the rehearsal room. All the windows were open, and she remembered seeing swallows swooping in and out of the room.

The conductor held up his hand and the music began. Tam had sat listening, drenched in it. And just as she was enveloped and lost, there had been a sharp tap. "Enough, gentlemen!" It had stopped.

David had done just that. Whatever had started to happen between himself and Tam, he had stopped it sharply; he had called "Enough!"

*

One evening, the shooting for the day over, she was on the beach when her father lounged up to her. He was in his *Tempest 72* costume, barefoot, in ragged white trousers.

"Three and a half minutes in the can to-day," he said briskly.

"And not a sign of Maggie Street either," murmured Tam. "Could there be a connexion?"

"Poor old Mags," drawled her father. "I don't know why you have your knife in her. She admires you."

"Dad. It won't work."

"Pity. I thought I might soften you towards her."

"I can't like everyone and she gives me the creeps. Wherever one looks, there she is. She practically hangs like a bat from the sound boom."

"The word for her is ubiquitous," said her father, digging his toe into the sand. "I don't mind it. I like people to be keen."

Bernard came hurrying up.

"Sit down, boy, sit down. I don't want you wearing yourself out."

From the man who wore Bernard out for twenty-four hours of the day, this came as a surprise. Tam and Bernard exchanged glances as Bernard sat down on the sand.

"You must look after yourself, my boy. By the by, we need the reels early, Clive and I want to see them around eight before I have a bath. Then supper at nine. Order it for that time, will you, and fix about the rushes."

Bernard sprang up like a jack-in-the-box and hurried off. Her father watched him go, calling:

"Take it easy. Tam can drive herself home for a change."

Tam was tracing patterns in the sand. Her father said, "Peaky. You look peaky."

"Does that mean you didn't like my scene?"

"And sharp with it," he said, pinching her cheek. "You go back to the hotel and get some sleep, Tamara, and when you come down to dine with me to-night, wear the white dress. I'm damned if I know why you should be peaky," he added, studying her. "Look at me. I *glow*."

Tam took one of the unit cars and drove away. She was tired and nervous; she didn't want to go back to the hotel.

To-day she and David had sat under the olive trees during a long break in the shooting, and he'd talked about being a boy in the North and the pleasures of high tea. They must both, he had said, start a fashion for high tea during movie-making. Fish and chips and vinegar, served in papers of old script. "The bits they've made me re-write."

She thought of David's face. He had the beginnings of two lines down his cheeks; he was thin. It was an expressive face which reacted strongly, laughing loudly or getting energetically indignant. He was always quick and always clever. And when she thought, afterwards, of their conversations to each other, neither had said a thing.

As she drove along the bumpy road, she remembered the evening they had spent at the Gouriellis, and on an impulse, felt she wanted to see the house again. She turned the car and drove back along the lane towards a side turning. It was deserted, and the trees were turning brown, just as the vines withered more each day. She thought, "Did we turn here? Or here?"

Suddenly, as she slowed at the crossroads, she saw a familiar back in the dark. It was Maggie Street, walking with two men. Conscious that she couldn't be seen because of her headlights, Tam drove slightly faster. Her lights shone on Maggie, talking animatedly to the men who were listening to her with expressionless faces. All three, as if snapped by the flash of a camera at night, were frozen

77

for a moment in Tam's glance. The next minute she had passed and the figures were gone.

She peered round for the road which led to the Gourielli's house. She was lost. After twenty minutes she had to follow the distant lights of the village until she finally returned to the hotel.

She felt a sense of anticlimax. She had wanted to stop the car and look at the house, and perhaps re-create something about David and herself. All she'd done was to drive past Maggie Street.

She went to her room and lay down on the bed. Something kept buzzing in her mind. Maggie Street and the two men . . . they weren't local people; they certainly weren't tourists; and they weren't part of the unit; and yet . . . they were film people; she was certain of it. To anybody in pictures, somebody in the same job was unmistakable. What was Maggie doing with film people who were nothing to do with *Tempest 72*?

At nine o'clock, wearing the white dress, Tam came down to dinner. Her father and Clive were already on the terrace, Clive in a high-necked black sweater, tired, her father in a white tropical dinner-jacket, fresh.

"Snap," he said. "Good together, aren't we?"

His dinner jacket was made in the style of motion pictures of the 'thirties, and suited his black hair and excellent shoulders. He had an uncanny sense of dress, seeming never to bother about clothes, yet always, in a new style or an old, managing to make everybody else look dull.

"Clive and I are quite pleased with the rushes," said Robert Waring, surprising Tam by breaking his usual impenetrable silence on the matter. "Yes . . . we're quite pleased."

"They need some chopping," said Clive.

"Chopping?" said her father sharply.

"No one would chop you, Bobbie," murmured Clive, speaking as if he would rather show the entire amount of film being shot, perhaps 16 hours before cuts, rather than risk losing a second of the star.

"Quite right. Bernard isn't eating with us, by the way,

78

Tamara. He's gone to have a meal with some of the others."

Robert Waring knew that actors like attention; he used Bernard to supply it.

David did not join them either.

Her father chose carrot juice for all three of them as a starter. Clive remonstrated, pointing out that the theory that carrots were good for the eyesight went out in the Battle of Britain.

"Did it? I daresay you remember," was the reply.

"We're both too young to do that, I'm glad to say," lied Clive. "No, Bobbie. I'm having a martini."

Tam loyally gulped the carrot juice and asked Clive if Maggie Street had a job.

He sighed. "She keeps on dropping outsized hints at your father and me."

"Which we've decided to ignore," added Robert Waring. "Why do you ask? I should have thought you'd be pleased the poor thing's out of work."

"I don't see why she's got to nod and beck at Maggie Street merely because the woman spends her time buttering you up, mate," Clive observed.

"That butter, as you call it, is appreciation of the arts," replied Robert Waring. "However, even the best butter won't get her a job with our unit. We are not giving her one. Why did you ask, Tamara?"

"I saw her this evening before supper. I'll swear she was with motion picture people . . ."

She told her story. There was a silence.

Clive asked her to describe the men again. Tam, with the actress's sharp eye, did so.

She looked from one to the other.

"What's up? You two look a bit odd."

Her father laughed.

"That's because we've been hoping Maggie would go and it sounds as if someone's taking her off our hands. Now food. That's what we need."

The meal of fried octopus, followed by peppered steak, was eaten by the three with appetite. Tam did not mention

Maggie again: more talk of her would bore them. When Clive and her father were together, in any case, they amused each other.

As Clive was served with his spiced steak he observed: "By God, it's lucky we have good digestions."

"I'll tell you something. Bryden hasn't," said Robert Waring with relish.

"Why do you think that!" said Tam, laughing. "He eats like a horse, and, as well, he's only twenty-six."

"Age has nothing to do with it. Have you ever seen him chewing magnesia tablets? I am sure he has a supply in his pocket. You must have noticed him nibbling them, as you are always with him," he added, without a hint of meaning.

"Of course he doesn't chew magnesia!"

"I am sure you're wrong. Besides, why shouldn't he have indigestion? A stomach-ache can make an artist's fortune. No-one with a good digestion could write the bitter stuff Bryden does."

"Yes, it is bitter," Clive agreed. "It comes from somewhere. Why not from the heart?"

"It's bile. Those big speeches are bilious. Did you ever read the Kamoritz book on digestion and the creative faculty?"

Clive drooped his eyelids. Tam guessed that it was he who had lent the book to her father. Probably yesterday.

"The bit you'd enjoy is Chapter Twenty," said Robert Waring. "I think it would interest you, Clive. Remind me to lend it to you."

Tam was now sure the book was Clive's.

"You can skip through it too," said her father swivelling round and catching her eye. "We'll forgive you your ignorance because you played quite nicely to-day. You were softer. Do you agree, Clive?"

"She's very soft. Specially in a bathing suit," said Clive.

Robert Waring examined a peach as if it were Tam's performance.

"What we were discussing was the connexion between

stomach and art. Bryden has bile. Some actors and writers have no guts at all. Clive! How can I enjoy my food when you keep looking at the sky. Are you a clerk in the Meteorological office?"

"The weather fusses me."

"There are forty million stars from where I'm sitting. In any case I always have King's Weather."

When the meal was finished, Clive said he must leave them. Her father disliked anyone going before he did : "I take it you are going up to your room to spend the night with a telescope and a barometer?" he said sarcastically.

"It's just possible."

Robert Waring snorted but Clive shook his head and said "Don't tempt the Fates."

Tam and her father remained at the table. The candles had burned low and there was nobody left in the restaurant.

"Film directors," her father said, "are all bound hand and foot to their damned cameras. Letting the machine be the boss. What a mistake. Well, well, I suppose we must go to bed. Come up and say good night to me, Puss."

They went up the stairs together. Saying good night to her father did not mean the conventional exchange used by other daughters still living with their parents. Her father often liked a talk or a tease or both. Tam thought, you couldn't treat him as an ordinary parent. He was so strong that it was like deciding how to "treat" a North Wind.

In his suite, her father threw himself into a large chair and indicated that she should take a footstool. He liked to see her at his feet.

Through the open windows, she thought she heard a far-off grumbling sound.

"Not a word. Not a solitary word!" said her father, putting his hand on the top of her head and pressing it down hard. "If you mention the weather, Tamara, you can leave my room immediately."

"I wasn't going to."

"I am relieved to hear it."

He sipped some milk.

"That young man is in love with you," he said suddenly.

She started.

"And I don't approve," her father added.

"I don't understand . . ."

"You're upsetting him."

"I don't think he's upset," she answered faintly.

He laughed.

"I gather you don't fancy him much?"

"Dad, there's no point in talking about it. He isn't interested and neither——"

"Isn't interested! He hasn't been able to take his eyes off you for months."

"Dad!" she exclaimed. "How can he have loved me for a long time when I only met him five weeks ago!"

Looking up, she saw her father with his head on one side.

"Aha, so that's how the land lies. Bryden, eh? Our friend with indigestion. Well, well."

"Dad, I am not in love with David and he isn't in the least with me so *please*!"

"Not in love with a Waring! Why in heaven's name not?"

She couldn't help laughing.

"Monster. You're a monster."

"A *sacred* monster. Now I have two pieces of news for you, so let's desist from talking about the fascinating fact of whether men are, or are not, in love with you. You gather by now that I myself was referring to poor Bernard."

"Yes. Bernard is a bit fond," Tam said cautiously, and to get her father off the whole subject she said: "What about the two pieces of news?"

"Ah yes," he said. "Let's start with your playing. Don't tense up like that and don't look hangdog either. To-day's rushes have quite a lot of close shots of you. Your Miranda is working: you're not half bad. The other day there was one little scene you played with me and I actually let you steal it. Just go on like that."

She shut her eyes and gave a sigh of pleasure. It was the first time she'd been happy since David had kissed her.

Her father looked down at her and said approvingly:

"That's right. That's the way to feel. And here's the second piece of news. Your sister Candida will be here to-morrow."

*

Next day dawned cloudless, the sky tinged with pale apricot pink. The shooting started earlier than usual, and the technicians, who often seemed so slow to impatient managers worrying over the budget, actually hurried so that the scene was set, and rehearsals were ready to begin, by half past eight in the bright sun.

Maggie Street arrived just before the first rehearsal. She was wearing a navy blue suit, her hair screwed on top of her head in a bun. She looked business-like and ready for a hard day's work. She strode up to Tam, fitting a cigarette into a long holder.

"Haven't seen you for days. Any sign of Sir?"

"He's making up."

"I'll pop my head round the door. It won't be the first time, as I used to be his A.S.M., remember?"

Bernard was standing beside Tam, and he murmured : "Perhaps I had better . . ." and followed Maggie's retreating figure. A moment later, to Tam's surprise, Maggie was back, angrily brushing Bernard out of her way. He said something to her in a low voice and Maggie answered loudly :

"Okay, okay, I know when I'm not wanted, but to *order me off the set*! What's so sacred about a shooting? There are fifty people here, aren't there? And I've known Robert Bloody Waring since he was in small print at the bottom of the bill. Don't bother——" as Bernard added that he would go and get her car, "I don't need a wet nurse."

She flounced off.

"Golly!" said Tam.

"It was bound to come," answered Bernard. "Sir suddenly blazed at her like a man with a machine gun; the poor thing was riddled with bullets."

"I don't think she's a poor thing, she's hard as nails," Tam said, watching Maggie backing her car expertly and driving away.

She remembered the two men she had seen with Maggie last night. Her father had never ordered Maggie away until now.

*

Tam was made up and in costume waiting with the other actors; the clapper boy came forward and chanted his familiar litany. The camera rolled . . . Rye Ingsoll and the crew stood around . . . her father seemed to grow taller, he walked slowly down the beach towards the sea with the camera following . . .

The world suddenly changed. For the first time in the weeks of shooting a dark cloud moved across the sun. Clive shouted :

"Cut !"

The sky darkened with extraordinary suddenness, huge clouds shaped like ogres came from behind the mountains of Sicily, there was a splitting noise of thunder, the downpour of rain followed instantly as if a bath were upset over them.

Chaos followed.

The camera operator, his harness jogging, ran for cover, people dashed through the sheets of rain rescuing props, recording apparatus, equipment. Actors covered their hair and faces.

Bernard bent to pick up a shooting script in the mud, the red ink corrections smearing like blood.

Tam, running for shelter, looked back for her father. He hadn't moved. He folded his arms, letting the downpour sweep over him like a man under a waterfall. The rain plastered his hair, he lifted his face to let water course down his cheeks.

Bernard rushed down the beach with a huge scarlet and gold umbrella, and Robert Waring, relinquishing his role, allowed himself to be escorted to a small deep cave which opened in the rocks nearby. Clive, Rye and the camera crew, as well as other members of the unit who hadn't crowded into the van, were already huddled in the cave like damp cattle.

"Don't say it !" said Robert Waring, as Clive handed him a cheroot.

"Perhaps we should shoot in the rain," suggested Clive without conviction. "Rye says if we light *behind* the rain we can't see it, and we'd certainly get some interesting shots . . ."

They moved farther into the cave together, followed by Jilly, the continuity girl, who held a gas cigarette lighter up for illumination; its straight flame shone down on the star's dripping face.

Tam's costume was wet and chilly as she moved farther into the cave to avoid the rain beating in through the entrance. She shivered with cold, and then she felt her shoulders wrapped in something. She looked round gratefully, expecting Bernard.

It was David. She thanked him, conscious that the coat was still warm from his body. They stood staring through the mouth of the cave at the sea lashed with rain. The arc lights and cables lay everywhere; it was like a deserted circus.

"Sir says your sister is coming to-day."

"Yes. We're excited about seeing her," she replied. She thought "Why do we have to talk like this? We might as well say nothing."

The cave was crowded and as somebody passed by with a "Sorry, sorry," she tripped and fell into David's arms. He put them out to catch her, and as he clasped her, she felt him tremble.

They drew apart self-consciously, as Robert Waring emerged from the cave's dark interior, still illuminated by Jilly's lighter.

"Come along, Tamara. We are going to meet your sister. Bernard!" he added, looking out into the storm. "Run and get the car and drive it down on to the beach to pick us up, will you."

*

At the hotel, Tam and her father pelted across a courtyard bouncing with rain, up the stairs and into the Waring suite. A girl, standing by the window, ran towards them.

Candida threw herself at her father, Tam hugged her sister, Robert Waring gripped them both so tightly that they had to break away, gasping.

85

When the kissing stopped, he went to the bedroom to change and Candida rang for a bathrobe for Tam, saying:

"I wouldn't like to be you if you start a cold now!"

"Oh—help——" grunted Tam, as her head was smothered by Candida using a rough towel and rubbing so hard that Tam's teeth knocked together.

She came back into daylight with hair in spikes and ears scarlet.

"Aren't you glad I'm back?" said Candida, sounding like her father.

Robert Waring lounged in, barefoot, wrapped in a white dressing-gown and smoking a cheroot. The Warings sat down on the settee, and he put out his arms and pulled them to him on either side so that they huddled like passengers in a crowded bus. The people he loved must be close. Sometimes at home he would put both feet into Tam's lap; once he sat so close to Candida that she fell off her chair. When his daughters kissed him, he always exclaimed with satisfaction: "Quite right."

The room was almost dark, black clouds covered the sky and the rain continued to fall in torrents. Through the open windows came a smell of drenched earth which mixed with the cigar-smoke in the air.

"Well, Candida? Did you miss me?"

"All the time!"

"Hm."

His elder daughter had a manner which won everybody. It was so melting. Later on they discovered her independent spirit and felt cheated; all except her family who rightly assessed the mixture in her nature. She was considerably taller than Tam, with thick fair hair and long eyes. She had enough of her father's looks to be beautiful, and the actor's narcissism in her was the radiant desire to please. Her voice was moving, yet when you listened, you did not know exactly why.

"You're thin. Positively scraggy. Your idea or theirs?" asked her father.

"Theirs."

"Well? What about the picture?"

86

Candida was more interested in talk about her appearance.

"Wallace, that's the director you met, Dad, said he knew exactly how the girl I was playing should look. He said she was a 20th century version of some Italian primitive. He had his beloved primitive blown up life size and then kept popping into my dressing-room and comparing her face to mine. Then he'd lop calories off my lunch."

"*What* about the picture?" repeated her father, who was the only one allowed to wander from the point.

"It was all right. I suppose it was all right. Wallace was marvellous to work with, I *really* liked being with him. But mine wasn't the main role, Dad, as you well know since you chose it for me. She's only in the second half of the movie."

"And walks off with it if the role is played right, which we trust it is," he remarked. "My idea of a role. A stealer. You signed an excellent contract too."

"The money looked enormous . . . but I do hate talking about it," sighed Candida. "I sound stuck up. I suppose it's because it truly embarrasses me."

"A first-rate way to keep up the price."

Candida talked about Hollywood, Tam listened and was silent. Robert Waring was reflective. He had spent long periods there when he was younger, sometimes starring in one American picture after another; in one way, his world fame was due to those years. But he had not gone back there, and now only accepted occasional roles in epics rarely made in the United States, but shot in distant countries which provided a number of things: hot sun, forests, deserts, swamps, wild country—and cheap labour into the bargain.

Waring had become interested in making pictures for other reasons than those of the star giving his art to the world. He wanted his Royalty ensemble to make films so that they would become known to a wider public as well as making more money; some of the company were already playing together now in *Tempest 72*, the first part-Royalty film venture. Because of this, Hollywood seemed remote.

87

It was amusing to listen to his daughter talking of the place: he doubted if it had changed much. He asked if the wars between millionaire production heads and their directors were still waged to the death. Did people lower their voices when speaking of money? Were writers still used, six at a time, like canteen cooks making stew? He was surprised when Candida did not know, in detail, the answer to every question. He attributed to his daughters the knowledge and perspicacity of somebody of his own age.

"And how's that old fool Steve?"

"Very attractive," said Candida promptly.

"How's his billing? Smaller?"

"Right at the top," said Candida who, unlike Tam, never gratified her father's thirst for bad news about his contemporaries.

"He must be sixty if he's a day."

Candida giggled. She said everybody in Hollywood admired Steve, and that in her own picture he had acted a tragic scene wonderfully.

Her father listened with disbelief:

"Tragedy, indeed. Steven's an undertaker. His idea of a tragic scene is to look as if he's measuring you for your coffin. What about that head? Some maddened actor playing opposite him put it in a vice at one time. That's why it looks like this . . ."

He put his hands on either side of his temples and pushed as if the skull were going to crack, at the same time compressing his face into a long mournful grimace. Candida laughed.

"It is Clive's birthday to-day," Robert Waring said. "I'm giving a little dinner party for him to-night. Candida, child, now that you are here, you may sit at the top of the table . . ."

"But Dad, surely you . . ."

". . . On my right hand," he said, raising it like a bishop conferring a blessing.

*

The girls went to Candida's bedroom to unpack the pile of suitcases. Tam, always interested in new clothes, took out

88

a number of Candida's American dresses, arranged them on the bed, and tried some of them on. She stood in front of the glass, studying the effect.

"How'd you like me for a 'seventies version of one of the 1930 girls . . . Carole Lombard, for instance?" she said, picking up a large fur muff and putting her cheek against it. She gave Candida a swimming look.

"We could have a present-day version of Tamara Waring, perhaps?" suggested Candida.

Tam put down the muff. Her face became rather blank.

"Yes. There's her," she said.

Candida, watching her, said cheerfully: "I'm so out-of-date with the news. What's been happening while I've been away?"

Tam did not meet her eyes.

She picked up the muff again and clasped it to her chest, like a hot water bottle.

"Maggie Street's been here."

"No!"

"Do you like her? I can't bear her."

"I've never fancied her much," Candida said. "I was always rather sorry for her. At a distance."

"There wasn't any distance about Maggie when she was here," said Tam with emphasis. "She hung round the unit all the time until Dad got rid of her to-day."

She sat down still grasping the muff, and told the story of Maggie Street's angry exit. Candida was intrigued and asked, couldn't she perhaps be up to something?

"What about some scandalous bit of information about Dad? She could be after that."

"Candy! One has to have *orgies* to make the dirty mags. Clive said the other day that people were running out of things to do that scandal sheets would even be interested in. And Dad's so—well, isn't he!"

"I didn't mean dirty stories, Tam, I meant information. Production companies sometimes hire spooks—spies—that's what they told me in Hollywood, to find out what rivals are up to, report on scripts and casting, even on budgets. Perhaps a rival lot have been paying her to report on 72."

"Maggie the spy!" said Tam, laughing and not amused.

She fidgeted. Candida waited. Tam said suddenly :

"Miranda's going all right. But one or two scenes aren't jelling and they worry me sick."

"Most people aren't pleased with their work when they're at it. I always loathe mine," Candida said.

Tam wasn't listening. She continued to fidget with the muff, stroking it, ruffling it.

Candida thought her younger sister was changed. Of course actresses fretted over their work, sometimes couldn't sleep over it, but Tam looked curiously absent, as if her feelings were held in suspension rather than troubled. Candida had always felt protective towards Tam, and amused by her sister's pushing nature. She liked to watch the ambitious little thing wheedling and coaxing and losing and winning. This was different.

She said :

"Have you been falling in love, by any chance?"

Tam looked up but said nothing.

"Is it that gorgeous Peter Moneto? Girls are always falling for him. He's dynamite."

Tam burst out laughing.

But even as she laughed she thought it would be no good to tell Candida who it was. What could Candida do? Only comfort her. Only say kind well-meaning lies.

"Of course I haven't fallen for Peter. And now *you* must tell me every word about Hollywood because I plan to be offered a huge part there any minute," said Tam.

*

The bar of the Caesario hotel was plushy, the chairs covered in embossed white and gold leather, the heavy wall-coverings of dark red velvet. Above the bar, glaring down with eyes like gimlets, was a portrait of a nobleman who had once lived in the house.

Tam and Candida, who had spent hours dressing for dinner and listening to the rain, came into the bar in search of Bernard. They found him at the bar counter writing busily.

"I do think you could stop and pay some attention to us," said Tam. He looked up to see her standing beside him. She was dressed in yellow silk, with glass beads sewn round a high collar, and wore her air of expecting his love and attention.

"Hallo, Bernard darling," said Candida, drawing up a stool beside him and bending to be kissed. "Is the rain going to stop? Are you shooting to-morrow?"

"We're still hoping. Sorry for bringing all this stuff with me, but the weather has put the schedules right out and we're hours and hours behind," he said, shoving his papers into a folder and ordering drinks. Bernard loved all actresses and worshipped the Warings but he looked regretfully at the folder.

"It serves them right for shooting in the autumn. It's my bet these are the equinoctial gales," said Tam. "We should have done the picture two months ago."

"It's much more complicated than that, Tamara, as you know perfectly well. It hinged on when Sir, Clive, Rye, Peter Moneto, and half a dozen others were all available. In any case, David wanted it to be shot in the autumn. He said it was the right season."

"Even Hollywood has heard of David Bryden," said Candida. "Which is pretty staggering. They usually only admit to knowing names which appear nine foot high in the credits. I'd like to meet Mr. Bryden."

"And so you shall," murmured Bernard, "because here he comes on cue."

Candida saw, with surprise, that the man coming across the room was handsome; she always expected the opposite in writers. As he walked towards them, she thought that his lively face probably concealed a shy, anxious nature.

When they shook hands he said :

"I've seen everything you've done, I'm a passionate fan."

"And I wish I was in 72," she said.

"Shakespeare would have given Prospero two daughters if he'd met you," he answered promptly.

Candida laughed, glanced across to Tam, and found her questions about her sister answered.

*

When they crossed the restaurant to go to her father's table, which was set with more candles and places than usual, Tam was conscious of the storm still blowing out-

91

side. Filming made one truly concerned about the weather —a new anxiety. She could see the rain coursing down the great glass windows of the restaurant, and beyond them the dim shapes of branches streaming in the wind. By contrast indoors seemed warmer and brighter than ever.

Talk during the meal was vivacious, her father and Candida were both on form; Tam was quiet. She was sitting between Bernard and David, and both of them talked to her at intervals between listening and laughing at her father's spirited evening performance.

During the dessert, a flan of wild strawberries, Robert Waring bent forward, so that everybody at the table would pay attention.

"David, you know, I've been thinking a lot about Prospero these past few days. Don't you think it would be interesting if he had a bad leg?"

There was a hushed silence.

David signalled a look at Clive who did not signal back.

"What's that old-time expression for a bad leg, Clive?" asked Robert Waring. It was one of his gags that Clive was many years older than he was.

"Gammy leg?" suggested Clive.

"Exactly. How expressive. Prospero must have broken his when he was shipwrecked. Those rough seas and sharp rocks. His dinghy was stove in. A bad leg will alter him; make him more complicated. A favourite character of mine has a wooden leg now that I come to think of it."

Robert Waring stretched out one of his magnificent legs, clad in white silk trousers, and just missed tripping up the head waiter.

David said carefully : "What favourite character is that, Sir?"

"Long John Silver. There's a man I've always had a fancy for."

David was not at all amused. "But Prospero is a scientist. A magician. Perhaps a bit of a saint . . ."

"Tell you what. I prefer a pirate."

David and the star began to argue; the rest of them looked on.

When David began to get heated Robert Waring smiled

92

blandly. "Mustn't bore them, must we, boy? Come along, Candida, let's see if they taught you to dance in Hollywood. You never could dance as well as I."

The music was a souped-up version of British pop, and on the square of floor in the centre of the restaurant a few couples were moving around, more interested in talk than in the dance. When the Warings stepped on to the floor, both with the curious radiance of actors, the dancers looked gratified.

Clive watched them for a while. Then he turned to David, whose face was set.

"It's no good, mate. You're not going to win this round."

"But it's balderdash! The Prospero character can't be mucked about like that! It's adding slapstick to serious drama."

"And haven't you noticed that when Bobbie's acting serious stuff there are always times when it has a definite tinge of farce?"

"That can't be true!"

"It is true. He never feels that the two things should be kept apart. They aren't in life, he says. Also, he knows both are in his own personality; sometimes he allows them to get too close and they run into each other. One of his performances in Ibsen illustrates my point. At matinees with a lot of school children in the house, he always got a roar of laughter in the wrong place."

"Clive!" broke in Tam. "That simply didn't happen!"

"As you were ten at the time, darling, I don't suppose you were informed."

Clive rarely used such a dismissive voice, and she blushed.

"I directed your Dad in the Ibsen, it was *Master Builder*. He tried everything he possibly could to stop those kids laughing at that point. He would experiment with different entrances and exits . . . sometimes very quickly, darting across the stage, sometimes slowly, slipping unobtrusively round the edge of the proscenium. One afternoon he tried materialising, like an apparition, at the top of the stairs. They thought that hilarious. He used to get very cast down. He'd come and see me backstage, throw himself in a chair and say 'the little bastards laughed again'."

93

"But that was terrible!" exclaimed David.

"But that was *funny*," answered Clive, "because Bobbie is. He's a genius. He's full of the stuff of life, comic as well as bloody sad. *He* knew why those kids laughed. The effect he wanted was high drama, and he got it with the adults, all that darting about thrilled them. They were spellbound. The kids just sat there guessing how he'd achieved the effects. They treated it as if they were watching a funny conjurer. Children . . . apart from Royalty . . . are the worst audiences in the world."

He looked from David to Tam. Their solemn faces made him smile.

"Anyway, Sir was having you on. As if he'd suddenly alter his performance and spring anything as earth-shaking as a broken leg on us. He'd have thought that angle up months ago, worked it so that it was an intrinsic part of the character. He's a joker. I'm surprised at you, Tamara darling. He can fool you yet!"

Just at that moment her father returned to the table, dragging his leg like a wounded G.I. in an American battle movie of World War II.

David and Tam, embarrassed at Clive and Bernard's laughter, went across to dance.

A waiter went by, pushing a trolly on which was a large birthday cake for Clive, bright with wavering candles. Tam and David stepped on to the floor and the music began. It was years old, soft, very sentimental; the lights went down. Tam and David moved close in the dark.

"I suppose," he said, "I should have guessed he was fooling me."

"I didn't. And I've known him all my life."

"Oh, you! You pretended, just so as to keep me company. You have a warm heart."

He put his arm round her shoulders. She closed her eyes and thought "If only we could stay like this . . . like this . . ." The music was weakening. She could smell the soap or eau de cologne that he used. Its smell reminded her of kissing him.

"Italian syrup. Arrivederci Roma and come back to Sorrento. Do you like it sweet?"

"Not much."

"Nor do I." He pressed his cheek lightly against hers. They danced for a while, very close and not speaking.

The music ended, the lights went up and they stood blinking. They trailed unwillingly back to the table, hand in hand.

The candles on the cake were blown out and slices were cut and lying on plates. Robert Waring was smoking a cheroot, Candida and Bernard having coffee.

"You are allowed a small piece of cake, about the size of a postage stamp. Clive, cut it for her," said Robert Waring. "That's right, swallow it down, Puss. The party is over. We need sleep. Candida looks all eyes from her journey this morning, and as for you, David, we will discuss my gammy leg in the morning." Robert Waring looked him up and down.

"There's a long shot when I will have to limp into the sea . . . we must talk about that."

"We'll have to shoot it again," sighed Clive.

"No doubt, no doubt. Good heavens, is that the time? By the by, everybody, Clive and I would prefer, if you happen to meet Maggie Street around, that you should use discretion."

"What does that mean?" asked Tam, fascinated.

Her father said airily :

"We've told her, not to put too fine a point on it, to get to hell out of the unit."

Everybody looked pleased.

"We're not very happy about Maggie being here at the moment," said Clive. "So if any of you see her—dodge!"

As they left the dining-room, Robert Waring walking ahead, there was a scatter of applause from the dancers. He waved.

Out in the foyer, as everybody turned to say good night, they noticed a group of people just arrived. Talking excitedly to the manager, they were drenched with rain, and dripping in pools on the marble floor. There were six of them, dressed in sailing clothes and oilskins, all with the reddened-brown faces of people who have been living on boats.

"We thought we'd never get to harbour!"

"Waves were ten foot high and trouble with the engine."

Finally, in a loud voice from a woman in red oilskins: "*I* need a bath!"

Tam turned to David and pulled a face.

"They're just the kind to make a noise. If they do it in the corridor outside Dad's room when he's trying to get some sleep he'll come out and shoot them!"

David didn't answer. He was staring at the fair woman in the red oilskin coat and Tam followed his glance. The woman, blonde and thirtyish, reminded Tam of an old-style comedienne in a musical.

"I must go," David said suddenly. He had gone pale. Without looking at her, he hurried away towards the side door which led to the garden.

*

Candida woke Tam at five thirty in the morning, and the moment Tam opened her eyes she noticed the silence. Candida said: "Yes. It's true. The storm's gone."

Tam yawned.

Candida said, "Sorry to wake you, darling, but I thought if you had a hot bath you'd feel better. I've run it for you."

Tam looked at her sister, thinking enviously that she looked in much better shape to film than Tam herself did. Candida was already dressed, in an almond pink sweater and trousers. Her hair was covered with a scarf patterned with letters of the alphabet. She looked composed. When Tam was in the bath, Candida came in and sat on the bathroom stool.

"Dad woke me nearly an hour ago."

"For God's sake, Candy! What for?"

"Said he wanted help."

"And did he?"

"No. I got up and bathed and dressed and went to his room and he was dictating his biog to poor darling Bernard. When I came in he inquired what I wanted."

"So you said coffee."

"How did you guess?"

"Dad just likes us all hanging around," said Tam, slowly soaping her legs. "If *he* happens to be awake, then every-

96

body has to be. He can't believe his luck now you're back from Hollywood and he's King twice over."

"For the time being, anyway," observed Candida.

Revived from the bath, Tam put on black trousers and a sweater, brushed her hair, didn't bother with her face since she would be made up directly they arrived on location.

Candida said, "Dad did his limp again after you went to bed last night, for Bernard and me. He had us rolling about. Your David Bryden didn't like the gag much, did he?"

Tam pulled on a knitted cap.

"He isn't my David Bryden."

"Could be if you wanted."

"He's just the author and we get on," Tam said, looking at her sister, daring her to take a step forward.

Candida merely said :

"We need coffee, and here it comes, I can hear it clinking in the passage."

Down in the foyer Bernard was looking ghastly and ghostly, his sweater, knitted in lambswool and coloured a spooky grey making him fatter and paler than usual. Tam had her usual pang of affection at his unfortunate choice of clothes.

He was relieved when the girls came down the stairs. "We're setting it up at the Roman temple again. Clive wants to do Scene 40 as the dawn comes up. The birds fly at dawn."

"They might not fly when you want them," said Tam.

"They fly left to right across the island," Bernard replied. "I checked. The hotel manager told me to ask a local farmer. Nice man, but his accent was impenetrable. He kept miming the dawn. I'm crossing my fingers I understood him and got it right."

Candida considered asking if the birds were under contract, but it was a pretty weak joke and Bernard and Tam were neither of them in very good spirits.

"You may not be needed right away, Tamara," Bernard said as they drove along.

"Surprise," she said ironically, but her voice was equable

and Candida thought the philosophical tone new from Tam, one of the most impatient people she'd ever met. Candida herself had discovered that the mental attitudes needed for making pictures had to be physically learned; in a way they were as difficult as acting itself. You had to school yourself to doing nothing, to being made up and dressed in costume and left, apparently forgotten, for hours at a time. You had to remain calm, relaxed, ready to play if you were needed, ready to stand in intensely hot lights or shiver in damp winds at dawn.

Tam was quiet and her sister imagined she was thinking of the scenes they were going to shoot to-day. Tam was not. She was thinking of David. She thought of how they'd danced and how close they had been. His face was thin, and when he'd pressed it to hers, she had felt his cheek-bone against her cheek.

"When he touched me last night he was trembling," she thought. "Darling David. You were trembling. And I'm going to see you in five minutes' time."

The car drove across the hilly island roads, bumping through a village where the only house alight was the baker's, where preparations were going on for the morning's batch of loaves. At last the road ended, and there on the grass by the temple were the vans, drawn up like the trailers used at a fair.

The chaos of filming was everywhere, cables tangled across the wet grass, arc lights pushed together among heaps of wooden boxes, recording apparatus, sound booms like outstretched branches of trees. Lights suddenly blazed, illuminating with dramatic brilliance a group of sundry people talking together. As suddenly, they switched off again and momentarily everything was dark. Men passed to and fro with walkie-talkies, or carrying step-ladders.

Bernard parked the car under the trees, and went off to look for Clive, taking Candida with him. Tam waited until they were ahead, and then went to find David. She pulled her cap over her ears in the cold dawn, and threaded her way through the crowd. The ground was thick with mud, and soon the soles of her thin shoes were caked, and her feet were freezing cold.

David wasn't by the make-up van, and she couldn't find him with Rye Ingsoll. She looked round for the familiar figure, with its bright red hair. Bernard came up.

"Tamara. Have you seen David? Sir wants him."

"He's around somewhere, I think," said Tam, deliberately casual. As she spoke, the arc lamps sprang up again, bathing the broken stone pillars of the temple in a false glare of noon.

She left Bernard, and went on looking for David in the crowd; perhaps it was too early and he hadn't arrived. She felt absurdly disappointed. She went over to a group of people by the canteen van; they were drinking coffee, the mugs steaming in the chill. Jilly, the continuity girl, handed one to her.

Clive called : "Tamara, I want you, my darling." He beckoned.

She went over to him.

Clive, wearing a huge windcheater with a hairy fur collar, looked down at her. Her face was tense, at odds with its youthful lines and freckles. Clive thought of the emotions he wanted to see in that earnest 20-year-old face. As in her father and sister, there was a moving quality in her. She could be hurt and, he was glad to note, it showed.

"We aren't shooting your scene for a little while, but I want you to think about it. I thought we'd try something slightly different to-day. Suppose Miranda is fighting her feelings . . ."

Tam listened as he talked, concentrating and nodding, her eyes on the muddy ground. Clive squeezed her hand and said "Good girl" and went back to Rye Ingsoll who was composing the first shot, having the lights moved around.

Tam sat down on an upended box and drank her coffee. Dawn was beginning, and the actors stirred in its pale light, looking at the sky.

Her father came into view, dressed in Prospero's long green robe, which swept to his feet in majestic folds. He moved slowly, carrying a tall staff wreathed in fresh seaweed.

The lights, like instruments joining an orchestra, lit one

by one, bathing him in subdued brightness and making the green robe luminous.

"Silence. Rehearsal starting *now*!"

The rehearsal ran for barely three minutes, and then stopped. Robert Waring and Clive conferred, Rye Ingsoll joined them. They stood looking critically at the lights, which apparently Waring was objecting to.

Candida came up quietly and stood beside Tam.

"Tam. I've something to tell you."

"What's that, darling?" said Tam absently, as she watched her father.

"David's gone."

Tam looked up.

"Gone? Where? I've been looking for him all over the place. Has Dad sent him off to do something else with the script; he is too bad!"

"I mean he really has gone. Left the island."

Tam just stared.

"That's impossible."

Candida spoke fast. "I know, it does sound absurd but he really has gone. He got a cable last night, apparently. Work or family troubles or something. Clive told Dad a moment ago. He said David was terribly upset. He had to hire a boat to take him over to Sicily to get a plane. He left messages apologising to Dad and everybody. As there's only two more weeks on the location left, Clive says he won't be back."

Candida bent forward to take Tam's hand. Tam wouldn't let her. She stood up and walked away, tripping over the cables that snaked through the mud.

4

After David left, the intimate circle of the unit closed as if he had never been part of it. Clive received a letter from him saying how disappointed he was that he couldn't return to the island. Something tiresome and important had come up in London. When Clive mentioned this to Robert Waring, the star was withering: "And *what* is more important than the picture? How does he know we won't re-write his screenplay, now he's out of the way? If I were a writer, I'd be sitting on the set at dawn every morning with my script and a loaded gun."

Tam was glad that she had to work hard, get up each morning early and go to bed worn out after shooting all day long. She was glad that work, and the actor's natural ability to cloak feelings, could hide how much she was hurt.

The last two weeks of the shooting were a long struggle with the weather. There was a sort of poetic justice in *Tempest 72*, in which the elements played so big a part, being hounded by storms. Winds sprang up, blowing gusts of leaves which scattered across the scenes being shot; each leaf had to be swept away by a man with a broom who stood by as if doomed to sweep away autumn itself. Rain beat down on actors shivering in thin costumes. Trees chosen for a particular shot were bent double by sudden squalls. When the film needed the sea to be a glittering calm, it showed its teeth and turned dirty grey.

Every night nobody talked of anything but the next day's weather. Bernard was in touch with the meteorological office in Naples, and spent a lot of time on the telephone "nattering," as Robert Waring described it "with some fool with a spy glass on a Cathedral roof."

The star took the bad weather personally, and his daughters saw him shaking his fist at the sky.

"And don't think," said Candida keenly, "that he doesn't mean it."

*

When Tam wasn't working, she brooded over David, wondering again and again why he had gone. She was sure it was something to do with the people who had arrived at the hotel on the first night of the storm. His face had looked tense and he'd gone white when he had caught sight of the fair woman; and he'd left the island the following morning without seeing Tam again.

She had spent hours—days—with David and she'd often noticed that he never talked about women. He had told her about his boyhood, and the poorish school he went to; he was dismissive about his family like many men she knew. He talked about his time at University; he talked, now and again, about his work.

Once when they were on the beach alone she'd said :
"What about birds?"

"Birds?" he'd repeated, looking vaguely across the sand where a large seagull walked, leaving a pattern made by its pink feet.

"Oh, women, you mean! I love them. They have a great effect on everything I do."

Giving an agonised groan he fell stiffly on his back in the sand, his eyes shut and his toes turned up.

"What's that supposed to mean?"

The body stirred.

"I'm demonstrating how easily I'm overcome by one glance from a female."

One glance at another female had certainly sent him scurrying. Tam thought about the woman, who was still at the hotel and whom Tam occasionally passed in the entrance hall. She was silvery-blonde and seen close to had a metallic confidence. She must spend, Tam thought cattily, a lot of time and money on her face; it looked too cared-for. She wore dashing, over-youthful clothes.

Tam asked Bernard about the sailing people and he sighed.

"One's an industrialist, soap or margarine, who tells me he met Sir at a City dinner last year. He's on at me to fix a date for drinks. I warned Sir who's been very slippy so far."

Tam lingered, although Bernard had begun to work at his schedules again.

"What about the woman with fair hair?"

"She's the wife of the soap and marg. I met her in the bar when he was trying to pin me down. She's all right, if you like that kind of thing. They own the yacht, which I'm told is now repaired so they'll soon be leaving."

That evening, Tam and Bernard were driving back after the day's shooting when the sailing people drove away. All Tam saw of the woman was a neat fair head and a girlish jacket.

During dinner, which he was having with his daughters alone, Robert Waring threw a newspaper on the table.

"Well, girls. What about that?"

Candida picked up the paper and Tam bent close. An article with a black headline said:

"*Two Tempests and Two Stars*. An interesting battle is being fought on a small island off Sicily said to be the origin of the island on which Shakespeare set his play *The Tempest*. Sir Robert Waring heads the new Clive Diamond production of *Tempest 72*, being shot on the island. It is a mod version of *The Tempest* by playwright David Bryden, 26, which interpolates some of the scenes from Shakespeare's opus. But Steven Farmer, 45, British star with 20 years of Hollywood behind him, has accepted Cosmopolitan's offer to make a Hollywood epic of Shakespeare's *Tempest* in its entirety. This film, too, is to be shot on the same island . . ."

"Old Steve as Prospero. Another undertaker interpretation for the fans," Robert Waring commented.

His daughters were silent.

Candida was shocked. Her father was too arrogant and too famous to admit it, but it was a blow. Clive's production was limited in money and time; it was also a risk, for it was a prestige picture, breaking new ground. But a great Hollywood epic, if it worked, could spin money; "if you spend it, you make it" was a much-used phrase amongst movie-makers.

"Maggie Street!" Tam suddenly spat.

"As you say. Maggie Street," agreed her father. "Spying out the land, sending reports on how our picture was going and just what a good location we'd found. She actually made tapes of some of the scenes and mailed them back to Hollywood. Quite the secret agent."

"How on earth did you find that out?" asked Candida.

"It's surprising what you can accomplish with a crisp bank note," he said coolly. "I can see you are both going to ask me what I do next. The answer is, drink my glass of milk and have an early night and I advise you both to do the same. Bernard will be keeping us informed if there's any more in the press. There will be. Well, I'm off. Good night, loves."

He kissed them impartially and strode away.

Tam and Candida finished their coffee and went up to their rooms in a depressed silence. Just as Candida was turning off her bedside light, there was a knock and Tam came into the room. She was wearing a short striped dressing-gown and her legs were bare : she looked all of 13.

"Do you think David had anything to do with all this and that's why he disappeared?" she said.

"Don't be a prize idiot," snapped Candida. "How could the writer of one picture conspire with a corporation to film something that spoils his own work? You're talking like a stupid child. That boy going off unexpectedly has thoroughly upset you. The fact is, this place is unlucky. The weather's hellish. Your boy friend disappeared without a goodbye and now we have a rival picture on our hands and probably journalists upsetting Dad. I'll be glad when the location work's over and we can get home."

*

It was the last day and the last hour of shooting on location, and the bad weather had disappeared; it was sunny and still all day long, the sea like an emerald and the edge of the sky a pale apricot.

They had been shooting the last scene on the shore, and Tam, in costume, was sitting on the rocks, her part of the work complete. She had just done a re-take with Peter Moneto. Clive was setting up some long shots of her father against the calm bright sea. The beach was crowded with members of the unit; the camera operator, his camera strapped to his chest, was kneeling beside Rye Ingsoll. Clive stood with his hands on his hips, watching intently. The camera whirred. Tam, watching, was still and pin quiet. The noise of the camera stopped.

"Right!" shouted Clive.

It was over; the island with its flowers and storms; the unit encampment with its gypsy litter and crowds of technicians; the icy dawn waking and the heat of the sun at noontide lunch under the olives. Somewhere across the island was the Gouriellis' house and down the lane by the hotel were the branches that had brushed against Tam's face when David had told her not to love him.

"Tamara. Clive needs you for a final shot," said Bernard, breaking into her thoughts.

She started.

"I thought we'd finished. Is my costume squashed?"

She jumped up.

"You look beautiful," he said. Her reddish hair was gilded and her eyes were painted subtly to change the expression of her face. It reflected the island and the sea.

"One more little re-take, my darling," said Clive. "And then that's it. Stand by Prospero. That's right. Look up at him . . . yes . . . that's lovely. We shoot that."

It seemed to Tam, looking up at Prospero's face, that here in this artificial world was the only real truth.

*

It was bitterly cold in London. Only a few hours before, Tam and Candida had breakfasted in the sun on the terrace at the Caesario, shaded by parasols, and looking at a wall covered with the blue and white flowers of the morning glory. The garden had been buzzing with insects and thick with flowers. Italy, determined they should forget the rain and the mud, had put on her loveliest face, as if to say "How can you leave me?"

England, on the other hand, looked her worst, and the girls shivered as they climbed into the Rolls waiting at the airport to drive them home. Thinking back of the island, Tam wondered how different the studio work on *Tempest 72* was going to be. It was odd that from now on the rest of the same film, set in that beautiful lost place, was going to be shot in the dark, damp atmosphere of home.

Robert Waring was silent during the drive. He stared out of the window at the traffic and smoked a cheroot. He was in his closed mood when it was not wise to disturb him. The girls talked in undertones.

"Is Ben back from Washington?" asked Tam. Ben Nash was one of Candida's men—she had a considerable number but Tam always thought it was Ben she was in love with. Between pictures.

"Not for two more dreary weeks. He rang me every night in Hollywood, it was gorgeous . . . my lord, Tam, we need our fur coats, that's frost out there."

"Do not NATTER, women!" exclaimed their father suddenly. "Be quiet!"

A surprised hush followed.

"Bernard, telephone the studio and say I want to see the rushes with Clive this afternoon, and I mean every reel we've got. Clive and I are bothered about a thing or two——"

"Dad, do tell! What thing or two?" Tam couldn't resist asking, despite the warning signs.

"Tamara! I do not wish to hear that voice again for ten minutes. Candida, as the elder, I expect you to do more than discuss *apparel* and the undoubted grief you feel from being parted from that long-suffering admirer of yours." He turned a withering eye on her. "Occupy your time by reflecting on your career, which you have not discussed with me seriously for ten minutes on end since your return from Hollywood. I myself, however, consider that your future looks messy and requires attention."

Candida would have enjoyed giving a tart reply and could think of several. She gave him instead her dazzling smile.

"As for you, Tamara, immediately after luncheon you may go to the Royalty and join the Mime class; Hal takes them on Wednesdays. Also see Mrs. Richards about doing some more work on your voice; it must be extended. Motion pictures are bad for the voice, and yours is by no means on top form. Where was I?"

No-one would dream of telling him.

"Ah yes," he said, pleased at reducing everybody to respectful gloom. "Bernard, the reels will probably run six hours, and as well as Rye and the others, we may need Bryden. Where's he?"

Candida pinched Tam. Tam did not respond.

"I'll call him," replied Bernard equably.

"Do that. If he can't come to the studio, ask him to dine. I presume the boy is *interested* in the picture? For somebody supposed to feel so passionately about his work, he sloped off pretty quick."

"I believe he had some personal trouble," Bernard said. He always stuck up for anybody attacked by his boss, winning Tam's undying admiration and Sir Robert's unflagging annoyance.

"Gentle heaven, since when did personal trouble interrupt work? Suppose that I allowed these women to interrupt me?"

"There was a publishing contract he was worried about as well," added Bernard loyally. "He mentioned it two or three times."

This second reason seemed to Robert Waring even more paltry than the first.

"Am I not in his motion picture? Surely that is of more importance than bringing out some penny edition of his play to be performed at the end of the pier. If I can manage my contracts smoothly, why can't he?"

Robert Waring's management of his contracts was a family joke. When they arrived, his voice would echo through the house as he cried out that somebody was robbing him. He would then throw the contract at Bernard and forget all about it. What he invariably did remember was the exact figure of the Royalty box office returns.

The car stopped at the Hampstead house and the front door opened immediately: Harriet had been watching for them. She and the family's golden retriever Sheba came racing out together.

Everybody kissed everybody, while Sheba pushed her way into embracing groups, lashing their legs enthusiastically with her tail.

The girls went upstairs to unpack, followed by Bernard, the chauffeur and the Italian staff of three, all carrying suit cases and boxes. Harriet heaped more luggage in the hall; actors travel heavy.

Standing alone with his half-sister, Robert Waring looked round.

"The place looks fine, Harry. What about you? Have you been working hard?"

"Not a bit."

"Happy?"

"Now you're back."

"Of course! Felt lonely?"

"Why should I?"

"I can't believe the old place was the same without me. Or did you give a lot of parties for the company, and let them drink all my burgundy?"

"Every night," said Harriet.

He clapped his pocket, saying, "I thought for a moment I'd lost it. This is for you."

He handed her a packet tied with thin string. As she took it, Harriet blushed red through her olive complexion. She undid the parcel. Inside was a jeweller's velvet box, which, when she opened it, showed a gold bracelet with two charms: a heart set with pearls and an elephant with diamond eyes.

She was touched and shy.

"Dearest! How lovely. Thank you."

"You get the meaning, I trust," he said. "There's a woman I know who is a pearl of sweetness and an elephant of stubbornness. I wonder who it can be."

He burst out laughing.

The telephone began to ring. It would do this all the time that he was in the house; it would guess, correctly, when he had left, and promptly shut up, beginning to ring at the next place to which he was driving.

Harriet put the bracelet in her pocket and glanced round the room as her brother had done. She had enjoyed the respite while her family was away, and the chance to turn the house upside down, to have it painted and polished without her brother's demanding presence filling it.

Two years ago, through the sudden, at the time terrifying, appearance of a blackmailer, Harriet had discovered she was Sir Robert's half-sister: the illegitimate daughter of his father by a ballet dancer. At first Harriet had thought that to be the bastard sister of a world-famous star was something she must conceal at all costs, if she was going to protect her brother. She had disappeared from the Warings' house. But her brother had found her and brought her home, at the same time removing the blackmailer so successfully that the man, terrified, had left the country. Harriet's secret was turned into a triumph.

The Warings were always ready to laugh and cry: they were essentially actors. They were egotistical, impatient, emotional, selfish, passionate and loving. Knowing Harriet was theirs, they grew more demanding and demonstrative. In the past she'd served them and dodged their open arms. Now, exclaiming "Sister!" "Aunt!" they were not to be escaped. Harriet didn't exactly want to escape. She welcomed shyly the love poured over her, the generous admiration and arrogant questions: "What do you think—feel—believe? Tell us? Be part of us!"

But it was too late to alter and she couldn't unlock the doors of her nature. Robert Waring wanted to buy his half-sister expensive clothes, spoil and pet her and drag her out of the kitchen. Harriet wouldn't come.

"I like it where I am. Nobody knows your fads as I do. You just leave me in peace," she'd said ungraciously.

It was one of her brother's most quixotic and understanding gestures that he allowed her to stay in the kitchen wearing an overall; even though that overall was pink for high days and holidays.

*

Accompanied by Sheba, who walked close to her, Harriet went up the stairs. The sisters were busy unpacking, each in her particular fashion: Candida with method, Tam by throwing things all over the place.

Candida had nearly finished and was putting things neatly into drawers. She looked up.

"Darling Harriet. Did Ben call me from Washington?"

"Three times."

"How delicious," said Candida, with the expression of somebody certain of love. "I think I'll have a go at getting him now." She gave her famous smile, and went down to the hall. Robert Waring did not allow bedroom telephones except his own.

In Tam's room shoes flew and straw hats skimmed. Dresses lay on the floor like rags. Lumbering through the muddle and now and again sighing "Tamara, do be more organised," was Bernard. He looked a stone heavier from Italian pasta, and had the air of a downtrodden bear. Harriet noticed that Tam's manner to him was even more proprietary than before they had left England.

Tam herself was brown and had grown her hair. She had a new batch of freckles which covered her nose. Wearing a black dress, Italian shoes and black stockings, she looked beautiful rather than pretty.

"Your diet's very successful. Your waist is smaller than I've ever seen it," said Harriet.

"Yes, I am thinner," said Tam uninterestedly. "Where's my packet of surprises for you? I wonder if I stuffed it in Candy's case, my last one wouldn't shut. I must find it." She ran out.

When she had gone Bernard snapped an empty case shut.

"She hasn't been slimming," he said.

"But that's impossible." Harriet had lived for years with Tam counting the calories.

"She hasn't slimmed once," Bernard repeated. He looked at his watch. "I must go. I expect Sir will shout."

"I expect he will."

She didn't ask him what he had meant about Tam. Bernard walked heavily to the door and turned as he was leaving.

"She just got thinner," he said.

Tam soon came back with her presents—scent, gloves, handkerchiefs of real lace made by "a woman with a lot of wooden spindles." Harriet kissed her, and began to tidy the room. Pleased to be tidied by Harriet, just as she liked her hair done by Harriet, Tam talked about the film. She told the Maggie Street story. Harriet, who had read about it in the press, loyally prophesied failure for the rival picture.

Harriet finished the room, and Tam sat down in front of the glass and looked at her face dispassionately.

"I ought to do something about my nose. I can't understand why people have their noses fixed to make them turn up—I suppose they like that frivolous look. If I'm to play the big parts later on, like Hedda, I want mine *straighter*. Do you think Dad would object if I had it the teensiest bit straightened?"

"Don't fish."

"What do you mean? You know my nose has always annoyed me."

"It's a valuable nose," Harriet came up behind Tam and put her hands on the girl's shoulders, looking at the face in the glass, "I don't see why I should pander to your vanity but it's an endearing nose. You know it and wouldn't really change it a fraction of an inch, so don't treat me as if I were Bernard. You are speaking to your old aunt. Have you been falling in love, by any happy chance?"

"Happy!" echoed Tam. She bent and pulled Sheba's ears. Sheba sighed and put her head on the girl's lap.

"You sound as if it isn't going so well."

"Nosy old Harry, it isn't going at all."

"Is it Peter Moneto?"

Tam shook her head.

"Just what Candy asked. We don't all go for our leading man and mine wasn't mad about me; he was just crazy about himself."

Harriet's hands were still on Tam's shoulders; Tam shifted as if they were heavy.

"I suppose I'm in love. I don't enjoy it. It's David Bryden."

"Is it, now?"

"What do you know about him?" said Tam sharply.

"Only what everybody knows. That he's exceedingly talented and Sir admires him. I've seen two of his plays, and I met him a couple of times here at the house before you left for Italy. I should guess he's a tough young man. Quite difficult."

Harriet walked over to the window, standing in a favourite attitude with her arms folded. She looked down into the garden, there was frost on the lawn and the sky was streaked blue and grey.

"I haven't told Candy a thing," said Tam. "She'd only cheer me up just as she did when I was a kid. She's so resolute. Telling her one's troubles is never any good. She dishes out conversational aspirin. I can't tell her. She's too happy."

Harriet thought it was strange that Tamara still competed with her sister. Tam had always raced after her elder, trying to get level and then to overtake. And Candida had run looking backwards over her shoulder, stretching a hand to pull Tam with her. But you couldn't race with a sister to prove who was the happier person.

"I suppose you're going to stand there till I tell you all about it," Tam said, as her aunt continued to gaze out of the window.

"I don't give a damn if you tell me or not."

At Harriet's rude voice Tam said, more cheerfully, that one could not talk to a back. Harriet came over and sat down on the bed and Tam sat beside her.

She hurried through the story, now and again pausing to try and find the exact word to describe something. It was so difficult to say how it had been. Tam wanted to make her aunt feel and imagine it. Her talent could reproduce people and make them real as she talked, but she couldn't conjure the flowering branches, or the night sky.

"It was lovely and sort of mad, and then, do you know what he said when we were kissing? He said 'don't love me.' Wasn't it horrible?"

Harriet did not answer.

Tam described the people off the yacht, David's disappearance, and how it was all spoiled and finished now.

"Dad is asking him to dine, so I will see him again," she said. "And at the studios too, I suppose. I know it's over but I want to see him. He's so gorgeous, Harriet. Really."

"What was that woman like?"

Tam grimaced.

"It's no good my trying to be unprejudiced. I'm not. I thought she was hard as nails. She was very smart, rich, fair hair, one of those girlish faces that have got set, you know? Fascinating, I daresay. Sexy, I suppose. Anyway, she made my boy friend run away like a rabbit."

Harriet stood up.

"Don't worry. I'm not going to offer conversational aspirin," she said. "There's nothing to be done when you love somebody and he doesn't love you. I do remember *that*. I'd say you had better work damned hard."

The flat voice worked. Tam looked quite bright.

"Dad's sending me to Mime this afternoon," she said. "He says I need to be all limbered up for my next love scene. What a laugh."

*

Harriet was cooking in the rather magnificent Waring kitchens that evening : the "Italian lot" were there as well, busy and voluble. Harriet's instinct told her that her brother was likely to return unexpectedly for a meal with a lot of people . . . it was one of his less endearing habits and Harriet usually guessed right. He expected food, as in a German fairy story, to appear on a table from the floor when he said the magic word.

She had begun making an apple flan, of the kind made in France with syrup and confectioner's custard, when Ventura, the young Italian girl, nudged her.

"Don't be a nuisance," said Harriet, not bothering to look up.

Another nudge was followed by a burst of giggles.

"For the love of heaven——" began Harriet, and glanced up into the inquiring face of David Bryden. She recognised him at once although she'd only seen him across a roomful of people. His bright red hair and lively pale face gave Harriet a shock; she had forgotten how handsome he was.

"We've seen each other before. You're Tam's Aunt and I'm David Bryden." He shook her hand. "The front door was open and I followed my nose towards the kitchen. Please don't tell me to follow it out again."

"Mr. Bryden——"

"David, please! Tam has told me all about you. I've been commanded to supper with Sir and I came early hoping to catch Bernard, but there isn't a soul upstairs. Is this what we're having to eat?"

"Take your fingers out of my sauce!" Harriet banged his knuckles hard with a wooden spoon, and then apologised in confusion.

He said, "It's my fault but it smells so good, and when I'm hungry my manners go," adding pathetically, "I only had cheese and an apple for lunch."

Harriet relented and told Ventura, who was giving him come-on looks, to make a "very small" sandwich. When David had wolfed it, Harriet took him upstairs to the drawing-room and poured him a drink. She was about to leave when he said:

"Do stay."

"I have work to do."

He was sitting on the arm of the settee. Round him were the furnishings, paintings, silver, of a room belonging to a famous man. Harriet thought they suited David Bryden.

"You only want to go back downstairs so you can give those nice Italians hell," he said. "I recognise the tyrant of the kitchen."

"That's right."

"Sir upstairs and Harriet downstairs. What a combination."

"Shocking."

"Your Italians need liberating," he said. "I shall write them a manifesto. Perhaps I'll get them all jobs in some smart restaurant in Islington."

"You keep out of my kitchen. There's no liberty when I'm around."

"I love a woman without a conscience. Go on, admit. You prefer cooking to talking to me. Now I prefer to keep you here, and your duty as hostess makes it difficult for you to leave me. Who's going to win?"

"I'm not very sure," said Harriet, and thought, "Ah—poor Tam."

"How's Tam?" he said, the moment that her niece's name came into her mind. "And how did the rest of the shooting go after I left? It was maddening having to leave. The only news the studio seemed to know about was the number of minutes in the can. Is Clive pleased? How was the weather—I kept reading European forecasts which said 'storms.' Most of all, how about Tam's big scenes? It can't be easy being Sir's little daughter. Like being related to Mount Etna."

He glanced at a large photograph of Tam on a table nearby. She was peering from under a huge flat straw hat.

"Still, she's hardy," he said.

"The Warings all have backbone," Harriet replied.

He laughed.

"What a wonderful word; I bet they used that when you were at school. It isn't the back I am thinking about, Harriet. It's the id. A different shape altogether. More amorphous."

He stretched out his hand and drew vague shapes in the air, and just then the door opened and Tam, in a shiny macintosh and sou'wester, came in.

For a split second the man and the girl froze, David with his hand out, Tamara looking from under the brim of the childish sou'wester.

It was she who recovered first.

"Hi. I heard you were coming to supper. How's everything?"

"Fine. Great to see you." He was far less easy and this surprised Harriet, who had liked his self-assurance.

"As you're here," she said, "I will get back to my cooking. Your friend took me away from an apple flan."

"No, Harriet, don't go," Tam answered quickly.

"I dragged her up here by force," added David.

They were still looking at each other when Harriet went out of the room.

When they were alone Tam said brightly that they had flown in this morning and wasn't London horribly cold. Had David heard that they had only been two days over schedule; it was a bit of a miracle when you thought of the storms.

She talked in a fashion sometimes used in high comedy, her expression matching the delicate manner. And while she talked she kept seeing an image of a young-old woman with an over-cared-for face.

115

When Tam finished he didn't continue the conversation, but said:

"Tam."

"Yes?"

"I missed you."

He did not touch her; he remained quite a distance away. But his voice was like an embrace and she went slightly pink.

"Are you glad to see me? Have you forgiven me for rushing off like that?"

"It was nothing," she said lamely.

"That's right. Nothing."

*

The dining-room was lit by candlelight, Sir Robert's favourite illumination, which flickered on faces that were all vivacious, some beautiful, and most of them exhaustedly tired. Clive was there, and Candida in a pale blue dress, and Bernard, and Peter Moneto, and one or two actors and actresses of the Royalty company who were playing in the film. David, who was not tired, was in high spirits, and laughed at Robert Waring's good jokes and argued with his outrageous theories. He seemed, thought Tam, the most fascinating man in the room.

Her father looked keenly over at Tam now and again. She missed the looks.

The guests, as they were making a film, all left early— before ten; they would meet at the studio on the *Tempest 72* set at seven thirty next morning. David said good night to Tam in the hall, adding,

"I'll see you at the studio. We must talk."

Before she could say anything, her father shooed her upstairs, saying he wasn't hiring a Miranda with bags under her eyes. "Don't think there isn't a lot of the most important and difficult work to come. Some of your location stuff was child's play!" he called, as she hurried up the stairs.

After the guests had gone, Candida remained in the hall with her father.

"Come and amuse me," he said.

Candida looked at him, noticing that he had the rather satiric expression she called his "fencer's face." He linked his arm in hers and they went into the drawing-room.

116

"I suppose you've been spending your time thinking about that boy friend of yours," he said, referring to Candida's journalist friend Ben.

"He hasn't been taking up much of my time considering he's in beastly Washington at present."

"Do I hear a shrewish note?" inquired her father. They sat down on the sofa together.

"I know what you're thinking, Dad, and you can just *un*think it. I'm not giving up everything and everybody for acting. I rather love Ben. I might marry him."

"Of course, of course," was the soothing reply. He raised his dark eyebrows, as if surprised she should doubt the motives of her noble father, the parental saint. There were so many roles and quick changes. Only someone as fast-moving as he was could keep up with him. And then not for long.

She talked about her acting plans. Did he want her back at the Royalty? There was another film in the offing, what did he think? He listened and nodded, and once he said "Fine, fine."

"Dad! You are not listening to a *word* I'm saying!"

"No, as a matter of fact I'm not."

"Then don't complain that I'm not serious about my career. What have you brought me in here to talk about?"

"You are not the problem," he said.

"Is it about your picture?"

She had the sweet temper of a woman who from birth has put aside her own concerns for those of others.

"No."

He rubbed his chin reflectively. Candida waited.

"How do you find your sister?"

"Excited over the picture."

"So I should think. She's damned lucky."

"She knows that, darling. She's nervous."

"I am glad to hear it."

A small silence.

"A bit gone on the Bryden boy," said Candida.

Her father was looking at his hands. He spread them palm downwards and examined them. Candida had often

117

seen him do this . . . when he was drinking his morning tea; on stage during a pause at rehearsal.

She said tentatively :

"I don't know David Bryden at all, but it's a change, Tam having a soft spot for somebody. All she usually does is take up some actor she thinks needs a helping hand and drop him when he's okay again. This one's different."

"Why?"

"You know why. Because he's a marvellous writer. Because you admire him."

"Who says so?"

"You do," she said impatiently. "By producing his picture; and by wanting that play of his that he gave to the Royal Shakespeare Company. You can scarcely dismiss him as a nobody."

Robert Waring threw his eyes to heaven, and then said abruptly :

"Do you think she's in love with the boy?"

"If she is, she isn't telling. Not telling me, anyway."

"She may have told Harriet," observed her father.

"She usually does."

"Then it might as well be written in invisible ink for all the information we'll get out of Harry. Even I cannot extract things from the woman. She has enough of me in her to be able to thwart me."

Candida omitted to add : "So have I."

Her father looked down again at his outstretched hands.

"Do you ever feel there's something a bit odd in Bryden?" he said.

Candida felt a slight chill and said :

"What do you mean, darling?"

"I don't know, exactly. There's something . . . I sense it in his work. It is what gives his writing its bite. Something curious."

"Do you like him?" Candida said slowly.

"Very much, unless he argues with me," her father said absently.

There was another pause.

Candida thought of her sister upstairs asleep. Hopeful.

That was the quality about Tam that hurt you. She was hopeful.

"There's something ominous in that boy," Robert Waring said.

He looked up and caught her anxious look and smiled, the lines creasing at the corners of his eyes.

"Never mind. I daresay I'm wrong."

It was a phrase he never used, and made it more ominous than before.

*

Tam was in her dressing-room, getting ready for the scenes to be shot in the studio that morning. The room was glaring with lights, and the same three attendants were there, the two girls and the man, who had dressed her and made her up on the island. But the feeling of the cramped gypsy caravan was gone. Her present room was spacious and well-organised, as was the whole studio where as many as three films were being made at the same time.

It took two hours for Miranda to be ready. Tam was docile. Now and again she said mildly :

"The eyelashes hurt a little," or

"This bit of hair wants fixing."

It was Shakespeare's not Bryden's Miranda to-day, in a costume of soft green silk, with heavy gold bracelets and bare feet. As the team studied her, she moved to and fro to see how the costume swung.

A head appeared round the door :

"Miss Waring wanted on set! Miss Waring please!"

She left the overheated room and went into the passage, out of doors into the cold daylight, across a concrete path between buildings like aircraft hangars huge enough to house jet planes. Down long stone corridors full of hurrying strangers, Tam finally arrived in a far studio, clanging with noise, which was the *Tempest 72* set. Everybody belonging to the unit, who'd worked on the island, was there : Rye and his camera operator, the studio managers, Jilly, the continuity girl, Clive squatting talking to the crew.

Standing alone in his Prospero costume, lights bathing him, was her father. In his hand was his heavy staff, and he slowly lifted and dropped his arm, up and down, up and down, to make the movement easy.

When Clive saw Tam, he smiled possessively. He came over to talk about the scene they were shooting this morning.

"I want you to play it as if you were uneasy, uncertain, like the scene you did on the beach. You're not sure about love . . . not sure he loves you . . . your emotions trouble you. You're thinking of him. Then, as your father speaks," he clicked his fingers, "you push the idea of love out of your head. It's hard but you succeed. Then," he clicked his fingers again, "over Prospero's shoulders, you see Ferdinand." Click, "You're back in the whole gorgeous mess again."

He repeated it, describing the brusque switching from one mood to the other. Click. You feel this. Click. You change to that.

As he talked the arc lights came up one after the other.

Two hours later the shooting stopped for a coffee break. Tam was cold with nerves, a usual reaction, and Bernard came up behind her and draped her in a travelling rug.

She snuggled into it gratefully.

"Bernard, be a darling and ask David if he can come and talk to me about the next scene. Perhaps he can help. I know we talked about it weeks ago."

Her mind was preoccupied with her performance, and she spoke confidently : David was somewhere near, part of the work, necessary to it.

"He isn't in the studio," Bernard said. "He was due an hour ago. I hope he shows up later. Clive wants him."

Tam's face didn't change.

"The disappearing act again," she said.

"I should have thought he'd want to be around, since Clive plans to cut one of the big speeches," said Bernard. "All right, all right, Tamara, the speech isn't yours!"

Later in the morning, Tam and Peter Moneto played their love scene. Part of the scene had already been shot on the island in the real setting of cave and sand. Clive wanted more close shots of their first embrace, of Miranda's face and of her father in the background.

It was curious to see the cave that actually existed on the island, and had done for thousands of years, washed by the sea and warmed by the sun, reproduced in an English studio. Its shape and form, cunningly made to resemble solid rock, was constructed of board and paper and a thin wash of cement. As she stood by the cave, Tam remembered the moment when she and David had fallen inadvertently into each other's arms during the storm.

The rehearsal was called.

"Silence, everybody! Silence at the back there! Rehearsal starts."

Bernard took the rug from Tam's shoulders, and she returned to her performance like a swimmer to the sea.

Peter Moneto was facing her, tall and slender, with a boyish face and a shock of hair falling into his eyes. He had a fashionable face, bony and rather wasted, with a curling mouth and a touching, vulnerable expression. His performance often seemed inadequate and small to the onlooker on the set, but on film it became just right, strong and mesmeric.

If Moneto had a modern face, Robert Waring had an immortal one. He was nearly fifty, yet he had the physical power to hold young people in thrall: his face was heroic, noble and sly. He could both tame a huge theatre audience, and muffle his art so that in film it swam to the surface only through the eye of the camera.

Peter Moneto put his arm round Tam and pulled her close.

Clive watched.

"Now a kiss. Good. Again. And another."

They shut their eyes and went on kissing.

Clive said:

"Not warm enough. Closer. Miranda, go weak, relax in his arms as if you are going to fall. Miranda . . . you've never had a kiss until now . . . the beginning of sex . . . the great moment . . . Good. That was good . . ."

For a split second, she thought of David. Her actress's instinct told her she must be Miranda, think and feel Miranda and that if she didn't, it would show in her eyes. But for that moment before Miranda took command a wave of sadness and want swept through Tam as she put out her arms and was passionately kissed by a stranger.

*

Her father sent Tam an invitation, via Bernard, to lunch with him in the studio's V.I.P. suite.

This was a suite of two rooms among the executive offices, which was kept for visiting grandees; great stars were entertained there, and so were financiers—stars in other galaxies. Royalty had been given tea there once or twice, and temperamental actresses had been escorted there to weep.

A light lunch, chosen by Bernard down to the crispbread and chicory, was laid in the small room, which had windows overlooking the concrete studios and a few trees.

Robert Waring was already seated when Tam burst in late because she had been wandering all over the studios looking for David.

"We are serving ourselves as I do not want us to be disturbed. Sit down, Puss, sit down. I realise you don't like being late for me, but I will overlook two and a half minutes." He pointed at an electric clock, large as a clock in a TV studio, whirring on the wall.

"Beef? Salad? What will you drink, Vichy?"

Tam meekly accepted the meal, which was elegant and meagre. She wondered why her father had invited her. She wondered still more where David was.

"I daresay you want to know why I invited you to luncheon," said her father, crunching a fresh radish.

She glanced at him brightly.

"No, no, girl, you can take *that* expression off your face for a start."

"I don't understand what you mean."

"I, on the other hand, understand what you mean only too well. You appear bright and attentive when you have other things on your mind. You use the trick far too often."

"Dad, I wish you wouldn't look at me as if——"

"As if I were a dentist deciding which tooth to pull out? That is the way I feel. Tamara, I don't believe you understand the relationship of father to child. And I'm not

122

alluding," he added, "to the absurdly-labelled teenage revolution. No teenager within living memory has ever revolted against *me.*"

Tam did not reply. She looked despondent.

"Are you listening to me?"

"Of course, Dad."

"Good. Then let us talk. You are my child. Young. Quite beautiful. Inexperienced. Satisfactorily under my influence. Until you fall in love——"

For a second, she was deceived. She looked at him fearfully, thinking it inevitable he should divine everything about her. "You fall in love because *I* decide that it is time—

"I do nothing but in care of thee.
(Of thee, my dear one! thee, my daughter!)"

Now he was speaking in Prospero's voice, and when he finished the speech she answered him as Miranda.

He began to talk of Shakespeare's *Tempest*, of Prospero's feelings at the event of Miranda's love. She listened silently. She forgot the room where she sat, the noise of the studio outside, she forgot that she was hungry and that she was sad. She listened to her father's voice, speaking poetic truths and setting poetic puzzles.

*

"Sir suggested that I should drive you home," said Bernard, as Tam came out of her dressing-room in trousers and sweater, her face white from the application of inches of face cream.

With the tensions of acting over for the day, her head ached and she felt a deep depression. When David had left the island she had been unhappy, but at least the situation had been plain and unarguable for there had been no hope. The sea divided them, and physical distance was a comfort. But to see him, and begin to hope again, and then to be cast down, was new. On the drive home she stared from the car window. The shops were cheerful with lights in the dusk and crowded with people. A girl swung by, hand-in-hand with a man, a mother bent over a pram. The real world was full of love, while she, in her make-believe kingdom, was cut off from it.

When Bernard spoke to her she was startled to see that they were already in Central London.

"I said a penny for your thoughts. Have you been thinking about the picture? If so, I'll shut up."

His face, kindly, fattish, was as familiar as a brother's.

"Do you think me pretty awful?" she said.

Bernard said, "Of course," in a voice that was good tempered and automatic: his stock reply to an actress who apologised at the same time as she asked for attention, generosity and his constant thoughts. But Tam missed the note in his voice and was merely relieved that she did not need to worry about Bernard. Like her father, she preferred her slaves at least to pretend to be free.

"Do you know what I think, Tamara?" he said, as the car crept into the curdled traffic by Hyde Park Corner. "You need a champagne cocktail. It is probably my birthday," he added, using an expression of Robert Waring's.

She wanted to refuse, but found that she couldn't. He drove the car towards the Ritz and saw a parking space at once, saying "that proves it's my birthday." He looked pleased as he walked up the steps with her into the hotel.

They sat in a corner of the room on high-backed seats. A fountain ran into a marble basin. The waiter brought champagne cocktails, fizzing under slivers of orange, and Bernard put the glass into Tam's hand and they toasted the new picture.

They discussed the music, which Clive wasn't sure about and wanted to alter. They talked about the publicity photographs, some of which Tam disliked because she said they made her look fat. Bernard disagreed. He switched to her father, and told her about her father's visit to the dentist recently; Bernard could always make her laugh. Reviving, she glanced across the room.

David was sitting with the woman off the yacht.

Bernard, his back to the room, was chatting about the rushes he had seen the previous night. "There's a long shot of Sir which is breathtaking, Tamara. Clive wants to cut it! He says it's distracting. Clive quoted his favourite chestnut about the bits of your own work that you are crazy about being just the ones you should throw away. You should have seen Sir's expression!"

Tam was an actress. Her face stayed interested and smooth while she felt as if somebody had put a knife into her stomach. She answered Bernard, and talked to him, and leaned forward listening to him, and still managed to mask her feelings and to watch David across the room.

David was in profile, smoking and staring at the ground, paying little attention to his companion.

It was not seeing David that upset Tam, but seeing him with the woman. In the flattering lights she had a girlish allure, and Tam was reminded that her features were very attractive. She wore a white suède coat which set off her fair hair. Now and again, apparently teasing, she looked over at David and laughed. He said something and was silent again, he did not smile once.

All the time that Tam sat with Bernard, she was half-watching the couple across the room. She thought "that woman's sure of him." It showed every time that she laughed, and he answered so sullenly, refusing to look at her.

5

The sun blazed on trees covered with yellow and orange leaves. It was quarter to eight on a winter's morning, a cold twin day to summer, with sharp sunshine and a clear sky. The clang of hammers on metal could be heard in the distance, carpenters were busy building sets, making stair-cases; in another part of the studios other carpenters were busy dismantling them. Voices echoed in empty spaces.

Up in her dressing-room, Tam's team of three were waiting. Her make-up girl pulled a broad elastic ribbon over Tam's hair, drawing it taut so as to leave Tam's face like an empty canvas. The girl, who had a quiet voice and manner, inquired, as she did every morning, if Miss Waring had slept well. Tam answered, as she always did, very well thank you. The truth was that she had slept less than two hours and was trembling with tiredness; thoughts of David had kept her awake and now and again in the dark she had begun to cry.

She sat quiet while the make-up girl worked at her face. She didn't look in the glass, because she wanted to think about David a little while longer; and she knew that when she looked into the mirror Miranda would compel her attention.

Averting her eyes, she asked herself how you could lose somebody twice who had never once been yours. David had warned her not to love him, he'd been a particular friend and no more. She must think herself out of him. He loved another woman who made him as miserable, apparently, as he unknowingly made Tam.

At last she did look at herself in the glass. The make-up girl knew her job, and the spell worked every day. Miranda stared from the watery depth of the mirror.

"A little more green . . ." the girl leaned forward to brush the edges of Tam's eyelids.

The hairdresser began her hair, and the dresser joined him. Tam knew them well now, they were good-tempered and efficient : friendly faces round her. But the strong eccentric personalities of backstage theatre were absent. Film people were businesslike and kindly but never a little mad. The dresser, a girl with long dark hair, helped Tam into her white costume. It had a stiff band of pearls round the hem, and rustled noisily. Kneeling on the ground, the girl fastened Tam's shoes. Tam went out into the passage, the pearl hem swinging like a hoop.

A huge globe of transparent Perspex had been made for one of the modern sets of *Tempest 72*. Clive, Robert Waring and Rye Ingsoll were in the centre of the globe, which hung as if floating about four foot from the ground. To light the globe properly had taken 48 hours and it now shone with a myriad irridescent reflections, like a great soap bubble. Inside this glittering sphere Tam and her father were to play one of Bryden's important scenes.

Bernard walked over.

"Rehearsal starts right away."

"But I'm an hour early," Tam snapped. He was surprised to hear her voice was trembling; he had thought he detected the same shaking voice this morning on their drive down but had decided his ears were over-sensitive, he was always conscious of nerves because he was always talking to actors. Now he was sure that Tam was strung up. Under the thin film of make-up her face was strained.

"You don't mind starting right away, Tamara? You usually welcome it."

"Of course I don't mind." She made an obvious effort. Bernard was puzzled as he walked away. An assistant director, with a reddish face and a hearty manner, came over to give Tam a chair. She sat down carefully in the stiffened costume.

The strong light in the Perspex globe shone on Clive and her father who were gesticulating as actively as vaudeville comedians. Clive indicated a measurement, her father indicated a larger one. What were they measuring, thought Tam. A close-up? An emotion? Everything in the world of motion pictures was exactly measured. Assistants would run up and hold a tape measure against an actor's nose, carefully gauging his distance from the lens. "You must step forward exactly one pace." "Bring your arms down an inch, your hands are not in shot. Bring your chin a fraction higher, move your head a little left . . ."

How did you measure pain?

The studio manager came up again and told her officiously that the director wanted her. Tam climbed slowly into the Perspex globe. Her father was dressed in his high-necked scientist's overall, and was made up to look sixty. Heavy lines ran down his cheeks, the face was brooding and withdrawn, his hair, brushed forward on his forehead, was a dull grey.

Clive, turning to Tam, began to talk over the scene. They had discussed it often before but it helped to repeat and remind her. He described Prospero, in the Bryden part of the film just as in Shakespeare's, coming to the end of his powers. Miranda was at the start of life and happiness. "When she talks to her father she must look brilliant . . . her face must blaze . . ."

"She's quite a dab at blazing," said Robert Waring. "Some of the family fire, mm?"

He was in a good mood this morning; he and Clive were beginning to be convinced that they had a success.

Clive spoke to him about a switch of mood that came in the middle of the scene. Her father listened intently. Tam's eyes wandered through the glassy walls of the globe. An arc light shone out across the studio, and beaming down, lit David's bright red hair. For a second, forgetting everything else, she saw only David. He waved.

"Ready, Puss? Don't gawp," said her father sharply.

Tam turned to him, taking a deep breath.

"Everybody quiet, please!" called a loud peremptory voice from the other side of the set. "Silence at the back, please. The rehearsal is starting!"

Robert Waring put out his arm and pulled her towards him, and looked down at her with swimming eyes. Then he turned slowly and stared through the walls of the bright globe.

"This is the finish of my work. It is ending."

"Oh Father, that's not true. Just because things change."

"You mean because you've fallen in love."

"Perhaps——"

"Cut!"

Clive Diamond, crouched on a stool beside the camera, said:

"I've had an idea, Bobbie. Could you already have seen Ferdinand over by the door before Miranda does? Prospero always knows when people are near long before they can actually be seen."

Robert Waring nodded; he altered back to the scientist with a single breath, looked over Tam's shoulder, and his large eyes grew larger—"Like this?" he asked, returning to a matter-of-fact tone.

"Great," said Clive. "Tamara, you see your lover quite a time *after* Prospero does. You're worried, you're puzzled, and then what your father sees communicates itself to you; you know it's the man you're wild about. Your face changes . . . you put your hands, clenched, on your chest, not romantically, not gracefully, clench them into fists . . ."

Playing the part of Miranda, Clive looked in the direction where David was standing under the arc. He acted the radiant look of a girl catching sight of a man she loves. He clenched his hands and put them on his chest. He said, in a choked voice, "Oh!"

Tam did the same. She did it twice.

"Right," said Clive. "Next rehearsal, everybody."

"Silence please. Quiet, please."

The words were like a refrain chanted in a courtroom. The holy hush of filming fell on the crowded studio. Technicians were statues by their lights and recorders, while the sound booms, like tree branches, thrust out above their heads. Men in overalls, holding light meters, tape recorders, screwdrivers or mugs of coffee, were immobile. There was complete silence.

"Rehearsal *now*."

Robert Waring pulled Tam towards him again, spoke the lines again, glanced over her shoulder; Tam followed his gaze, her face grew radiant . . .

David was looking straight at her.

For a second Tam's two worlds, the world of make-believe and the real world, clashed in mid-air. Reality was the stronger, the other world, fragile as a bubble, broke. She said loudly :

"Can I try again?"

"Okay, darling, relax for a moment." Clive's tone was like that of a gym instructor. Stretch. Relax. Up. Relax.

Her father murmured :

"Try it like this."

Effortless as a bird taking off from a tree, he turned from himself into a young lover, his face flowered, he looked tender and eager, and Tam saw his eyes fill with tears.

"See? That's the way the thing's done!" he said, switching off and grinning.

"I'll try."

"What do you mean, try?" he said, in a sharper tone.

"Pull yourself together. Don't play the scene as if you're
a love-sick parlourmaid."

Tam was too worried to answer, and merely returned to
the chalk mark on the floor of the set where she had to
stand.

"Silence, please! Shooting starts!" chanted the voice.

"Scene 303, Take One, Track One."

The camera began to whirr, Robert Waring lifted his
arm slowly and pulled Tam towards him. To the people
standing round in silence, the extraordinary quality of his
acting was a repeated miracle. He seemed to grow in stature,
his thoughts and physical presence to become one with the
onlookers.

"This is the finish of my work . . ."

"Oh, Father, that's not true. Just because things change."

Miranda looked up at Prospero. She stared across his
shoulder, her eyes swimming with intense concentration . . .

David was there. Still there. This time, in Tam's mind
the clash was more violent. To her own astonishment, she
cried out:

"I can't! I can't!" and ran off the set, sobbing as she
ran.

"Cut."

"Hold everything please, gentlemen!" Clive's voice was
cool. The camera stopped, tapes were switched off. Mechanics began to adjust lights. There was a small stir of
movement.

Tam ran out of the studio and up to her dressing-room.
Slamming the door, blessedly alone, she threw herself down
on a sofa in the corner. Five minutes is a long time to sob
your heart out. She was still crying when the dressing-
room door was wrenched open and a voice exclaimed:

"Stop that at once!"

Her father, still in his scientist's costume, still made-up
to look sixty years old, walked in roughly.

"Don't, don't!" she said.

"Don't what?" he asked contemptuously: "Don't spank
you? I ought to! Don't scold you? I'm going to! Do you
expect me to allow you to behave like this?"

He took her by the shoulders.

"Sit up, girl."

He sat down facing her. She continued to give convulsive shudders but her tears stopped.

"What is the matter?" he demanded.

"N-nothing."

"Don't be a fool. Tell me at once."

"I can't do the scene."

He folded his arms, as Harriet did, and looked her up and down with a sarcastic smile.

"Since when? Since five minutes ago?"

"I've lost my nerve."

"Don't mutter, speak up, speak up," he said. "Always speak clearly, Tamara, never mumble. Why can't you play it? What's the trouble?"

Silence.

He examined her, studying the face, smeared make-up, disordered hair and red eyes. She gave another shuddering sigh. Most men would have been moved by such youth and grief.

He sniffed.

"Now we'll go back and do it all over again," he said.

"I can't! Don't make me!"

"All over again," he said. "Go and do something to your face."

Years of obedience, an inherited devotion to the drama, worked in Tam. She picked up the puff and began to do her cheeks.

"Now the eyes. And the forehead. What a mess. Come here, Puss."

She came towards him but for the life of her couldn't help trembling. She'd known him since she was born. But he was a frightening man.

Suddenly he laughed.

"You look very funny. I wish you could appreciate the joke, and I daresay you will one of these days."

He put his arm round her and this time drew her gently towards him.

"You mean because you and that boy have fallen in love," he said in another voice altogether, the scientist's voice. He looked across her shoulder to the empty corner of

131

the room. This time there was no David. The world of fancy opened, strong and bright as sunlight. Tam found she could create the beloved young Ferdinand. Her face was full of love and happiness as she, too, stared at the empty corner of the room.

Dropping his arm, her father exclaimed:

"Gentle heaven, girl, what a storm in a teacup! You're not a bad little actress. I sometimes see myself in you. Only now and then, mind!"

*

They filmed the scene at once. There were four takes, but only because of a change in lighting. Tam played exquisitely each time. There was no sign of David.

"Break for lunch, please, gentlemen!" chanted the voice. Lights were quenched. Staff hurried to the canteen. Bernard came over to wrap the rug round Tam:

"I've reserved us a couple of seats. Hungry?"

The canteen was full when Tam and Bernard walked in. Four hundred people were eating hot lunch. The food was good and the menu varied—trout, chicken, mixed grill. Actors, electricians, prop men, carpenters, sat in groups talking and eating; the noise of voices was deafening. Bernard took Tam to a corner where he'd fixed a place for them. His manner was tender, rather as if she were recovering from an illness. Handing her a glass of orange juice he said:

"How's the temperament going?"

"Don't! I feel a fool. Furious with myself."

"I love a bit of excitement now and again," he said. "Well-behaved actors make it so tame. What I enjoy is seeing Sir throw things. He hasn't done it for months."

Tam was ashamed and relieved, for even as she'd run off the set, she had been horrified at her own behaviour. She knew other actors threw temperaments but she always thought them self-indulgent and was proud of her own professional skill and calm. It was ironic that Bernard believed her tears had been part of the job, as her father had done. They would despise her if they knew the truth.

Bernard carried their coffee to the "rest room," a large sitting-room on the ground floor. It was warm and well-furnished but it had the atmosphere of a station waiting-room; in it, idle actors hung around, journalists waited for interviews, business men talked together, publicity staff, photographers, and all the many people with business in film studios, came and went all day and late into the night. The room was almost empty at lunchtime. Bernard and Tam went over to some chairs by a window, and sat down.

Bernard said:

"We break at half past five to-night with luck. It's Sir's big speech this afternoon. He's been known to do some scenes in one Take, just like that. Marvellous!"

"Hi!" called a voice.

Coming across the room was David.

"Hallo, Dave, how did you think it went this morning?" said Bernard. "Nice to see you around the set again. Let me get you some coffee." With the good manners of a person who spends his life looking after others, Bernard went off, calling over his shoulder: "Black or white?"

David sat down beside Tam, stretching his long legs and looking over at her with an expectant smile. He behaved as if they were still the best of friends. Tam had been shocked and miserable when she had seen him with the woman off the yacht, and thrown badly off balance this morning when he had appeared in the studio. She knew she was being ridiculous and must get over it, yet she could scarcely bear to look at him.

"You are very beautiful in that costume," he said, "I haven't actually seen it before, though I remember Sara de Lullo's design. Poor girl, you were a bit upset this morning, weren't you? I know how it is; I've had fits of the same thing myself."

She stared at the floor and said nothing.

David lit a cigarette.

"I haven't seen you for an age, except the other night when I had dinner at your home and then we scarcely had a word. I meant to come to the studio yesterday but the publisher rang me. A lot of things came up."

"Oh, I'm sure you've many interests outside the picture!"

Her bitter tone surprised him.

133

"I'm sorry, Tam. I *wrote* the picture, and I'd hate you to think I don't grudge every moment I'm not here. I'd much, much rather be at the studio than arguing about a maddening contract. We must see each other. Have supper with me. What about to-night?"

"No."

He didn't understand, and Tam, used to her father's superhuman quickness, thought, "How can he be such a *fool!*"

He smiled, showing dimples like scars on either side of his cheeks.

"You know what? You're father-ridden, that's what. The tyrant is grinding you down. Of course you must come. I promise to get you home early. I'll whisk you off for a meal and you can be back to your virtuous couch at ten. I've found a new place full of students, you'll like it."

"No, thank you."

At last he really heard the note in her voice. Leaning forward, he took her hand and squeezed it, giving the hand a series of little kisses.

"Go on—you solemn old owl—let's have an evening together—we deserve it——" he said, kissing her hand as he might have kissed the little hand of a child.

"Leave me alone!" She snatched her hand back as if it burned. "I've told you I don't want to see you. Go away!"

Looking at her angry pale face, David also went white. They sat staring as Bernard came across the room, accompanied by a man with a beard.

"Good, we've got you both together, and Kim Brady would like some pictures. He could do them right away, couldn't he?" suggested Bernard.

Kim Brady was on a daily paper and was that rare being, a journalist Robert Waring liked. The only other one was Candida's friend Ben.

"Take the shots of Miss Waring. You don't need me," David said abruptly.

Bernard and Kim Brady were surprised.

The photographer peered into his lens.

"We do need you, Mr. Bryden, and I just snap away. It's quite painless, I promise."

"I said *No*!" said David rudely, and walked off.

*

The session with the photographer lasted over an hour, and it was not until Kim Brady had thanked Tam profusely, and gone off looking pleased, that Bernard said to Tam:

"*What* about all that with David!"

She replied, in a thin voice, that she supposed David disliked being photographed.

"He's objected before, now and again," Bernard said reasonably. "He always told me he thought the pix should be of actors, and that a writer's job was just to write the words. Fair enough. But this time I must say I was sure he'd change his mind."

"It's obvious. He didn't want to have his photograph taken with me."

"A writer who doesn't want his photograph taken with a Waring, Tamara, wants his head examined."

"Now, now, what are you two hobnobbing over?" asked Robert Waring, striding up with Clive, "Bernard, fetch Rye for me, will you? Clive, let's talk about the long shot of Tamara coming through the door. Don't you think if she *ran* towards me, it would be effective?"

*

Bernard enjoyed driving Tam home from the studio in the evenings; he looked forward to any time spent with her, even when she was morosely quiet. But when the shooting was completed for that day, Clive asked Tam if she would drive back with him and have a drink at his flat. Bernard watched Tam and Clive going away together, and then went through the empty studios to Robert Waring's dressing-room.

When people first met Bernard, they always exclaimed, with envy and sympathy, about his work: "You must be exhausted. I can't think you'll manage it for long." They could not believe that anybody would stand Robert Waring's pace. But Bernard had become in some ways another self to the star. It was remarkable to live with an engulfing personality and not be drowned. Bernard did so without difficulty. He was close to Waring; at his right

135

hand. He acted as a sieve for a thousand pieces of information, as second voice, protector, friend. Something solid in Bernard always kept him from turning into a slave. Even his weight seemed more than physical, and was a spiritual strength. People leaned against Bernard's character.

When he knocked at Robert Waring's dressing-room door, he heard the star's voice calling : "Come !"

Robert Waring was seated in front of the glass, removing make-up with large wads of cotton wool.

Not turning round but looking at Bernard's reflection in the glass, he raised his eyebrows.

"And now what's happened?" he inquired.

Bernard drew up a chair.

"It's probably nothing."

"Yes, yes, it probably is, but I want to hear it," replied Waring, looking at Bernard's face as a sculptor might examine some clay.

"I think it was David who upset Tamara this morning," Bernard said.

"Of course it was."

"But we all thought . . ."

"Leave me out of the crummy amateur psychology," said Waring, examining one of his eyebrows in a hand-mirror and muttering "A new grey hair; absurd; out with it."

"Perhaps David has offended her. He's a difficult so-and-so," Bernard said.

"The under 30's have got out of hand."

"Not when you're around."

"Ah. I know how to manage 'em."

Robert Waring finished his face, and began to brush his hair, which was curly and still streaked with grey powder. He wore a white shirt but had not yet put on a tie, and with his broad throat and bare neck and unbuttoned silk shirt, he looked a middle-aged, beautiful Hamlet.

"How do you like Tamara's playing?" he asked, in a pouncing manner. "Do you think she's any good? Answer truthfully. None of your judicious compliments."

"I think she's good. But."

"But. But. Dammit, Bernard, your sentences to-night are tiresomely pregnant. But what?"

"I think David upset her. I took her to the Ritz yesterday . . ."

"Oh, you did, did you, and what time did she get home?"

"For *tea*," interrupted Bernard, unmoved by his employer's manner. "David was there. He didn't see us. But Tamara saw him."

Robert Waring had stood up impatiently a moment before, but now he swung round. Was David alone? Did he talk to them? Bernard replied in his careful manner, describing the woman David had been sitting with. Robert Waring walked about the room for a moment or two.

"What was it I want to speak to you about?" he said suddenly. "Ah yes, the budget. Got the figures with you? I've been thinking about that extra three days production time and it seems to me . . ."

Bernard, from talking feelingly about Tam, suddenly found himself discussing columns of figures.

*

Clive Diamond lived in a skyscraper that had sprung up on the South Bank of the river. Tam knew its shape well, her father often pointed it out scornfully: "There was a rehearsal room on that site when I acted as a boy. Clive's taken a flat in that hideous contraption. He must be insane. I've told him to buy a house."

But Clive was a man on the move. He did his entertaining in restaurants, his talking in flats, either his own, or if he was in Paris, Madrid or Rome, those lent to him by authors or actors.

He whisked Tam up in a claustrophobic lift which set them at the top of the pinnacle.

"You live extremely high," she said, following the broad figure down the corridor.

"Do you like views?"

"I'm not sure."

"Let's see how you like mine."

He opened the door and stepped back for her to walk in. The flat, in darkness, was bright as day, for the whole of one wall was glass, framing a glittering panorama of streets and buildings, with the river gleaming like black metal.

"Spectacular, isn't it?" he said, switching on a light in the room. "See if you approve of the rest."

The flat was entirely black and white: white marble floors, white fur rugs, black furniture. Fixed to one wall was a tank in which fish swam through waving weeds. Fixed to another, as if it were a painting, was a piece of blue and black sculpture in a jagged design like an open accordion.

Clive pulled up a chair and poured her a drink, saying one glass of white wine wouldn't damage her performance, would it?

He sat down opposite and began to talk in his thoughtful lazy manner; she listened, wearing the concentrated expression that her father often ironically described as "holy." Clive talked about some of the key scenes that were to be shot in the coming week; he touched on Miranda's love scenes. Tam looked very religious indeed.

His expression altered and he said quizzically:

"Are you wondering why I particularly asked you here to-night?"

"Of course not. I know."

"Why, then?"

She looked at him with the solemnity that belongs only to the very young.

"I know some of Miranda needs deepening. To help me understand her, I keep thinking *back*, re-creating the time when she was a child."

"I'm sure your performance is right," he said. "Don't alter it. But go on thinking about it in depth: that can do nothing but good."

There was a long silence.

Tam thought "Perhaps I'm not here because of my work. But if so, what was I asked for? For sex?" The moment she thought of this he started to laugh.

"I wondered when we'd get to that," he said, reading her face, "No, I am not after you, luscious as you are. Not at present, anyway. That's a relief for you, isn't it? However, in a way you are right. I do want something."

"Anything," murmured Tam, hastily adjusting her poise. "That's nice."

He stood up and walked round the room, shifting things

here and there. A carved bird in stone on a desk. An egg made of agate. He picked up a holder for dice and rattled it for a moment.

"I want you to talk to David Bryden for me," he said, turning round. "Let me explain. He likes you very much— he's always telling me so, and I know he admires your acting, though we all remember that nonsense of his not wanting you for Miranda before the picture started. Now that's quite changed, and David's for you completely. That is why I want you to do some talking for me. It's occasionally difficult, you know, to get through to a man of twenty-five when one is over forty. Oh, I know your father never has any difficulty, but his technique doesn't work for me. I want writers and actors to see things my way but with their own eyes. Their view of my view, let's say. I can't dazzle them as Bobbie does."

"But I don't understand."

"I want you to make David see for himself that the best thing for him is to give his next play to me and your father."

"His next play!" exclaimed Tam. "I didn't know he had written one."

"Nor did I. He's secretive about his work and he never told me or Bobbie anything. It was my American agent who found out about it. Apparently David wants it done in California in some University theatre workshop there. The agent got hold of a copy of the play and sent it to me. It's very good. Your father and I want it."

As Clive went on talking, she listened with bewilderment. Why should David, on the verge of immense success, *Tempest 72* almost completed and the play he'd given to the Royal Shakespeare Company much acclaimed, want to bury his latest work in a graduate theatre in the States, when it could open with a brilliant director and a great star in London? He was at that point in his career when another success, quickly following, could establish him permanently. In any case, new work from an important new writer shouldn't be given away to a workshop theatre with an audience of fifty students; it should be fought for by producers as a treasure is bid for at Sotheby's.

"But David must have explained to you why he's doing it! What did he say?"

"Not a thing. Just told me to mind my own business."

"Charming."

"No, no, Tamara, I didn't mean he was rude. He was quite friendly in a harassed way. He made me wonder, from his manner, whether he hadn't got into some kind of mess and was keeping a bloody silly arrangement he'd made years ago. Creative people sometimes do that; they fix things up when they're starting and find themselves clobbered later on. You could say that there's no earthly reason why he shouldn't give his work away to a lot of merry twenty-year-olds if he wants to. *But.* And that's where you come in."

Tam devotedly admired Clive, as an actress would admire the director who had given her a great chance; she also knew how much he was valued by her father. But how could she do what he asked? She would fail and look a fool. David and she had quarrelled and he was in love with somebody else.

"It's hopeless; I really would be no good at it, Clive, much as I want to help."

He did not seem put out by the refusal, apparently he had been expecting it. He smiled slightly.

"You'll do your best for us, my darling, I'm certain of it. You must try and persuade him you feel as strongly as we do about his work."

"Oh, but I do! It's wonderful——" she began. "It's just that I can't——"

There was a knock at the door, and Clive said, getting up: "That's him now."

Before she had time to collect her thoughts, David had come in.

"Hallo, both." He gave them a friendly look, and Tam, remembering her own furious words in the morning, smiled back with constraint.

Clive said:

"Now that I've fixed this up, I'm off."

"Off! Where?"

"Downstairs, Tamara," he said, giving her a bland

look. "I've explained to David already that you feel as your Dad and I do about his new opus. And though he won't listen to us, he tells me he's happy to discuss it with you since you belong, as he puts it, to 'the same lot.' I am leaving you same lot together and going down to the bar. When you've told David all about our need for him, Tamara, and about his need for us, you can both come down and I'll buy you a good supper."

He left the room. They heard the click of the lift.

There was a pause, filled with the sound of traffic hundreds of feet below.

Tam said:

"What a setup."

"I thought it rather nice."

She wouldn't smile; she was nervous again. She found herself wishing she was as cool now as she was on stage, on set. David seemed to take something from her when he was with her; she felt constantly at a loss with him.

"I'm sorry I was rude this morning," she said. "Please forgive me."

"It's forgotten. I was rude too."

His unconscious manner hurt her.

"Clive wants me to persuade you over your new play. I wish he hadn't. I expect you have reasons."

"Yes."

"I feel a fraud. It's idiotic of Clive, he's been a director so long that he's started directing people when they're outside the studio."

"We're pieces of his chess game," David agreed. "Which suits the room, specially as you're in black. You're the black queen, the most powerful piece on the board."

He was relaxed and almost tender. When he looked over at her she noticed again the lines in his cheeks that had been dimples when he was a child, and the bright colour of his hair, which had always fascinated her.

"I'm not going to try and get you to change your mind about your play," she said. "So why don't we go downstairs and join Clive?"

"All right." He didn't move.

Tam said suddenly: "Why did you come here to be persuaded by me to do something after you'd refused Clive and my father?"

"I wanted to see you."

"Oh, don't be so ridiculous!"

Her sharp voice surprised him.

"How we do quarrel," he said, sighing and staring at his feet. "Of course I wanted to see you. I haven't seen you for weeks, except at that dinner crawling with people. And at the studio this morning——"

"When I told you I didn't want to see you again."

"I know. But who takes what a girl says seriously? Specially an actress playing a taxing part. When Clive and I were discussing the play and he said 'why don't you talk to Tam?' I thought, yes, that's just what I want to do. Talk to Tam. But not about my work."

He leaned across and took her wrist, circling it with his thumb and forefinger.

"Tam. I love your name."

She pulled away but he held her fast. She pulled again. Then she let her arm go limp and said in a low voice:

"Please let me go."

He dropped her wrist at once.

She said perversely:

"Anyway, I don't see why you don't give your play to Clive and Dad. Are you dissatisfied with the way we're doing *Tempest 72*? Have you any suggestions?"

"Don't use sarcasm, Tam, you do it very badly and it doesn't suit you."

"And behaving like a madman doesn't suit you!" she flared back. "Only a writer who is off his head would refuse Dad if he wanted his rotten old play. Oh, I admit you're clever. Yes, I know you are, very very. But how *dare* you imply that Dad isn't good enough for you!"

He stared at her with his eyes widened, and then he smiled. It was so sour that it changed his face. The look shocked her.

The expression slowly went, and he was once again the man she knew and wanted.

"Darling Tam. It's no good. I can't and won't tell you about the play and I can't and won't listen while you goad me. I am going abroad soon anyway, so let's enjoy this bit. A little of it, on the island, was lovely, wasn't it?"

"No."

She went to the window, leaning her hot forehead against the glass. Below her the city, miles and miles of it, shone and glittered.

He walked over and stood behind her, took her by her shoulders and turned her round. Putting his arms closely round her, he kissed her.

She thought that she would pull away; she thought she wouldn't let herself be violently kissed; but she'd imagined it so often, enjoyed the empty pretence of embracing him, that when it happened all she could do was cling and kiss in return.

"Dear girl. Beautiful girl."

He stopped, looked at her as if to make his feelings stronger, and began again. Tam finally pulled away and went across the room. She picked up her coat and clumsily tried to put it on. He followed her, wrapped the coat round her shoulders and wrapped his arms round her again, hugging her tightly.

"Let me go, David, let me go——"

"No, I won't, my darling."

"Don't call me that!" she exclaimed, this time getting free of him. "It's no good, I can't pretend I don't know about you. I saw you the other day, with that woman."

He had been about to put his arms round her again. He stopped.

"What do you mean?"

Tam was self-possessed again. She fastened her coat and looked round for her handbag.

"I saw you at the Ritz, two days ago, with the woman who came to the island when we were there. Bernard and I went into the hotel and we saw you. David, I *know*."

"What do you *know*?"

"That you love her. That's it, isn't it? She was the reason you suddenly ran off from the island; you saw her and the next day you disappeared. It must be because of something between you, you care about her. It explains everything. Even why you're taking your play to America. Everything."

"Maybe."

"Fine. Fine," she said. "Let's go down."

He came towards her and she said suddenly:

"Don't touch me!"

He took no notice of the cry, but folded his arms round her, rocking her slightly and kissing her, knowing she wouldn't resist. She closed her eyes.

He said, "I shan't see you again so kiss me, that's it, that's it. I don't love that woman, I detest her. And now I've lost you, I'll hate her more. Kiss me."

Then he said,

"Explain to Clive that I had to go. Don't come to the door with me, I couldn't bear it. Goodbye."

He went out of the flat quickly, slamming the door.

6

It was the last day of *Tempest 72*. The dome of Perspex was finished with, and so was the studio cave that imaged the real cave on the island. They would pull down the studio cave and store it in a warehouse, while the sea washed in and out of the real cave, as it had done for thousands of years before the actors came.

Tam and Peter Moneto had played a love scene; Prospero had set his Ariel free. The players had stepped, for the final time, into roles as easy to them by now as their own skins.

In the afternoon it was over and people around the studio came to say goodbye. Of the disbanding unit, some had already left for a film in Wales, others were starting at a new studio to-morrow.

Rye Ingsoll, going in a week to Mexico, asked Tam to a party; the make-up girl brought her a bunch of freesias. Tam went to her dressing-room to take off Miranda's costume for the last time, remove the make-up, and have her hair washed. She sat, looking at her face. Miranda had disappeared completely now; she was on celluloid, packed in metal cans, due for cutting, fixing, transposing, for the editing of film-making at which the director was God. It would be three more months before Clive's work on the film was over.

But Miranda had left Tam's spirit, and she felt hollow. For days she had concentrated intensely, immersing herself more deeply in the film than ever before. Her father, approving, had been particularly kind to her. Now the work was done, and she felt as if some support, strapped to her back, had been unfixed.

She brushed her hair, left her face without make-up, and slowly buttoned the shoulder of a dark dress which made her pale face paler.

There was a knock. Bernard looked round the door.

"Ready?"

"Just about."

"Want me to drive you home?"

"Please."

"You'll have plenty of time before it starts," Bernard said. She was not listening. She picked up the coat that her father had brought her back from Finland. It had a long thick fur trimming from neck to hem, and when he'd given it to her, and seen her wearing it, he had observed: "One day you may be able to manage Anna Karenina."

She pulled on the coat and glanced in the mirror.

"Before the party starts," repeated Bernard, bending to pick up her scattered belongings, books, gloves, scripts, the freesias . . . "The studio party. Now don't tell me you haven't heard about it because I can see your invitation stuck in the mirror. They're giving it for the picture, and a lot of V.I.P.s are going to be there. You know you love the big time. You'll enjoy that."

Bernard's voice reminded her of Harriet's, when Tam had been a small girl: "Home-made lemon curd for tea. You'll enjoy that."

"You know how good you are at parties," added Bernard, still in the same tone.

Both of them knew that at present Tam was anything

but good at parties, even at simple conversations with a friend. Tam said yes, she'd like to go home to change please. They went down the corridor together.

As they drove away, they were saluted at the gate by the commissionaire and waved at by two of the camera unit going into the canteen for tea.

"Endings are rather sad," Bernard said.

"Yes."

"Never mind. Sir wants you back at the Royalty, so everything will be starting again. The new season opens soon."

Tam thought with a jolt: "I didn't know." A few months ago her father's theatre, its changing plans, its chances for herself, its casting, hopes, fears, were her life.

"Sir's having a planning meeting to-morrow. Cross your fingers, you might get a nice line of parts, Tamara. So you cheer up," he said. "Did I tell you about Sir's argument with the TV people . . ."

He slipped into shop.

But as they talked, he looked pensively at the pale girl beside him, wrapped in her absurd coat. When she was happy, Tam seemed hard. Fortune's favourite. When she was sad, she was pathetic, a waif in rich clothes. It was this softness that touched him. They drew up at the Hampstead house and he switched off the engine and sat for a moment in silence. It was already dark.

Tam stirred.

"I must go, I suppose. I feel tired. What time does the party start, Bernard?"

"Eightish. They're going to show a new movie that's just come from Hollywood—a sneak preview. Then supper. Then a cabaret. Sir has been asked to appear. He says he might do his Buster Keaton; he hasn't decided yet."

"But is sorely tempted," she said with a faint smile.

Bernard leaned over and took her hand. It was cold and he rubbed it between his own. She remained passive, with the absent look he'd seen recently on her face.

"Tam."

She did not reply.

"Don't look like that!"

146

His voice wasn't the rumbling voice she knew; it was rough and unguarded and Tam was startled out of her self-absorption. For days she had only looked inwards, either at her work or at her thoughts. Now she looked at Bernard, using her senses.

"Bernard——" she said, leaning forward. He shook his head and put a finger across her mouth.

"Don't say it. I don't want to hear it. It was going to be very sweet and I don't want to hear a word."

"You don't know what I was going to say."

"Oh yes I do."

She bent forward, this time, and kissed him, and he said: "Not that either. I'm just around, you know."

He leaned across her and opened the door of the car.

*

The kitchen radio was playing pop and Candida and Harriet were drinking sherry. Sheba, under the dresser, was gnawing a large mutton bone. The Italians were out; Harriet had thought up a reason for giving them the time off. Candida was in jeans and Harriet's sleeves were rolled up. There was a holiday air.

Tam rustling in, wearing her dress made of silver fringe, was greeted with ironic applause.

"Who's it all for? Us?" asked Candida.

"It's for Clive Diamond. She's after the director," said Harriet.

"Harry, he's *forty-five*!" said Tam with amazement.

"I suppose it's for the party and don't take any notice of us, we're drunk. You look gorgeous; quite a knockout," said Candida, looking round for the sherry.

"But why aren't you dressed?" asked Tam; she envied Candida the jeans she was wearing and Harriet's company and the general air of festivity. The radio said "hallo hallo this is number two," and some voices began to sing "Freedom! Freedom! Di-di-di!"

"I'm staying at home with my old aunt and we're having eggs and watching TV," said Candida. "Ben is ringing me later. He's back next week, thank God."

"But how are you going to get out of the party? How are you going to get round Dad?"

147

"Get round Dad! Nobody gets round him!" cried a voice, "and what possible pleasure is there in drinking sherry in the kitchen?"

Robert Waring came through the doorway, dressed in his white dinner jacket yet with the annoyingly healthy air of having just returned from a long country walk.

"Girls! Don't mooch! Candida, what are you doing in those disgusting jeans? Why are you not dressed for my party? Don't tell me you can climb into your clothes in five minutes; I like a woman to spend at least *an hour* on her appearance when she is going out with me. I have noticed a distressing lack of respect for the big occasion in you recently."

He took the glass of sherry out of his daughter's hand and sipped it.

"While you are all here, I have a snippet of news. The Hollywood epic *Tempest*. Remember? I can see you do. I was telephoned by a feller in Beverley Hills to-day. It is off."

"No!" they chorused.

"Off," he repeated. "My most unfavourite actor, and, Candida, your dear friend, old Steve, had a flaming row with the director who has in turn fallen out with the Cosmopolitan boss. I believe he insulted him, in that friendly way of his. A familiar tale. In any case it was all going to cost far, far too much."

"So all Maggie's ridiculous spying was a flop, the old bitch," said Tam.

"That will do, Puss," said her father, delighted at her venomous voice. "Enough talk, we are wasting time. Candida, those jeans offend my eyes, off and change, please. Wear black, it suits your colouring. And do something interesting with your hair, girl."

"But Dad!" moaned Candida, "I can't go to the party. Harry's staying at home to keep me company."

Her father raised his eyebrows.

"Can't? Can't. Nonsense. Off and change. You've got exactly thirty minutes."

He pointed at his watch.

Candida hesitated.

148

"It wouldn't be any good telling you that my boy friend's calling from the States, would it?"

"No good at all."

"But I adore Ben, Dad. I want to talk to him."

"Then we will have the exchange transfer the call to the studios," he said impatiently. "Twenty-seven minutes." He pointed at the second hand.

Candida sighed.

"You win; you may as well know the truth, since you'll find out anyway. I can't go to the party because I've just been sent a script of *Aragon*, yes, the film you were in, darling, they're thinking of a new version and I might be right for Catherine. What's more, believe it or not, your old *Aragon* movie is on telly to-night. I've got to see it, haven't I?" she finished, shrugging wildly.

Everybody looked at Robert Waring.

"My old film," he said.

"Yes, Dad, nearly thirty years old and still pulling them! Clive rang me and said I was to be sure to see it and Harry's dying to stay with me and watch it too. Clive said you look killing in it."

"Killing?" repeated her father, frowning.

"All heavy eye make-up and cheek-bone . . ." said Candida, her voice trailing to a stop.

There was a tense pause.

"*Aragon*," he said reflectively. "Yes, I remember the notices mentioned my eyes. Catherine sounds a promising part for you, Candida, that's very perceptive of Clive. After you have paid your respects to the profession to-night, you may return early to see my picture. It is, incidentally, on BBC2 at 10.25 and Bernard can drive you home. In the meantime, the black dress, please."

She was pushed out of the kitchen, together with Harriet, both complaining loudly at the prospect of the party.

Robert Waring then invited Tam, "the only one with any sense," into the drawing-room. A fire was flickering in the grate, and a vase of large headed white chrysanthemums filled the room with the sharp smell of autumn.

Tam poured him a glass of wine and sat down beside him. He was pensive and said nothing as she looked at

him. Chance, pure chance, had given her father's face
its sardonic beauty, but its plastic quality was his own
doing; he used his face as relentlessly as a workman uses
his hands. Even now, in repose, it was startlingly alive.

He looked up.

"What are you thinking about, Tamara?"

"That you could still play the prince in *Aragon*."

"Of course I could," he agreed.

He eyed her.

"Candida's happy," he said. "That part should suit her,
as long as she doesn't moon too much over that boy friend
of hers. Emotions must be kept in check."

"Why?"

"Why?" he repeated. "My poor child, are you serious?
Emotions need to be checked and watched from outside, as
it were, so that we know how to handle them when we deal
with the real thing. The drama. What do you think would
happen to this family if I didn't do that? I'd lose my
audiences, be out of work, and the place would fall round
your ears. You don't know what it's like to be poor," he
added, lighting a cheroot.

Tam giggled.

He said: "And that's a noise I haven't heard lately."

His voice had altered, it wasn't the imperious or teasing
voice she heard every day; it was soft and it was loving.
When Tam heard that rare, moving sound, she turned
away her face and began to cry.

He put his arms round her and pressed her to him in
one of his strong, suffocating hugs; she leaned against him
and sobbed, and he patted her and petted her. After a while
the luxury of crying was over and she was quiet.

"Well, Puss. Now tell me what that's all about."

"Oh Dad!"

"Come along. Out with it."

"I love David. Did you ever fall in love with somebody
who didn't love you? I'm sure you never did . . . you
don't know how dreary it is . . . I don't want to gloom
round depressing myself and everybody else. I don't want
to want somebody who doesn't want me. Tell me——" she
said passionately, "how to learn to be miserable!"

"Suppose you start by telling me the tale from the beginning. I take it that Bryden's the chap."

"Yes."

"That's good."

"But he doesn't love me, Dad!"

"That's bad," he said, in his comedian's tone.

Tam actually smiled as she mopped her eyes; she told him the story, omitting nothing. She punctuated the tale with "Oh, it sounds stupid," "Well, you'll only laugh," but her father, who heightened ordinary talk with sarcasm or jokes, listened in silence. When she had finished he said :

"That's a rum tale."

"What do you mean?"

"It's intriguing. Here's a man who begins to fall for you. I'm not surprised, you're a Waring, and a taking little thing. And here's you, you fall as well. I can understand that as well; he's attractive and talented. A bit pig-headed for my liking but he feels strongly. And then up pops another woman; as a matter of fact, I remember her. Wasn't she this one——" He slicked invisible hair over his cheeks, drew a breath and, for one moment, *was* the woman Tam had watched a few days before.

"She had a mannerism—so——" he said, smiling and shaking his shoulders.

"Yes—that's her——"

"Rum," he said, returning to himself.

She leaned forward and took his hand. Like most actors, he reacted to a touch and moved closer to her.

She said, "You're so good to me. I know I've got to stop being dreary over him. If he wants another woman I'll have to get used to it and forget him. I can get over it. I know I can if you help me."

Her father let go of her hand, sprang up and walked over to the piano. He struck a loud chord.

"You mustn't be mawkish, Tamara. Use your head."

"That's what I'm trying to do," she said, chilled.

"What makes you think the boy doesn't want you?" he said, striking another loud dissonant chord with his left hand.

"I told you." She huddled back into herself again.

151

"And that story of yours shows he prefers the woman in the sailing gear? How can Bryden prefer a woman, forty if she's a day in spite of her girlie clothes, to *me*!"

"But I'm not you," she said, hearing the old familiar tone and sighing.

"Of course you are. You are my daughter. You have the magic. I don't approve of turning the heads of the young and you have a lot to learn but you have it, and should be on your knees in gratitude. No, no, girl, that man must love you. He's running away."

"From me?"

"For an actress supposed to be gifted with intuition, you're very obtuse. He's running away *because* of you. Yes, by God, and he's taking that play of his that I want with him. We must solve this, Tamara."

He banged the piano closed and began to rub his hands cheerfully.

"Dad! You're not going to try and get him back! I couldn't bear it."

"Come here."

It was a voice not to be refused. She went across the room and stood in front of him, and he looked at her with the satisfied air he always wore when he forced obedience from people.

He shook his head.

"That young man loves you. Do you think I haven't known it all along? It was I who sent you up to my room that night on the island, remember? You two had been quarrelling like cat and dog and it was quite absurd, when you were both interested in one another. I believe I can read the human countenance, child. Where do you think I get my studies? Bryden is in love with you and that forty-year-old teenager has a hold over him. Let's find out what it is."

"Suppose," said Tam in a low voice, "she's his wife."

"I had thought of that. Unlikely."

"Young men sometimes marry women in their late thirties."

"That one is in her forties. Yes, they do, and it usually doesn't work out. The point, Tamara, is that if he were married to her, it can't have been for long, the boy is only 25, isn't he? He would still love her if that were so. Marriages that break up because of a disparity in age take time. It's only over the years that the years begin to show. You don't know what I'm talking about, do you? Ah, here's your sister and your aunt and high time. Come along. Be guided by me. It is always best."

*

The studios were floodlit. Gates swung back, and Tam caught a glimpse of the linkman saluting her as the Rolls went by. It drew to a stop at a huge studio door, flung wide like the hold of a steamer which carries cars. Music and noise and light poured out.

"Come along," Robert Waring said, hustling them. "Harry, you stay with me. The girls can look after themselves."

He tucked his sister's arm under his, and walked into the studio. People came towards him at once and surrounded him in a circle, some kissed him, others were introduced. As he moved, the group moved too as if roped together.

Tam looked round, thinking to-night's party too large and indeterminate. She had always enjoyed parties, had known some brightened by furious scenes or dramatised by an actress taking off her clothes. Actors, tired and drunk, would sometimes insult each other, and often what was meant as an unforgivable row would turn into knockabout farce. To-night's party was just a jostling mob. Film people and business people drank together, technicians danced with girls in extraordinary clothes who to-morrow would wonder why someone hadn't given them a job after all. Directors and would-be directors collected in little knots, talking repetitive shop. People moved into profile so that photographers, edging through the crowds, would recognise them. The supper-room, decorated with garlands of artificial seaweed and lit like a cave, was laid for 600 guests.

Tam danced with Peter Moneto and drank champagne cocktails with Bernard. Candida, in the black dress insisted on by her father, was borne off by Clive to talk about *Aragon*. Tam heard her say: "The car's taking me home on the stroke of ten, Clive. I'm not missing a minute of the film!"

Tam, as she drank her champagne, was approached by one of the production staff of *Tempest 72*, a thin boy with crew cut hair.

"Dance with me," he said, rather bright on champagne. "Come on. Nobody else can have you!"

He tugged her on to the floor and into the beating music.

He was thin and short and danced well, his legs spidery, his face delighted at catching Tam as a partner. She was glad to dance in the violent movements of the music, to get hot and out-of-breath and just go on dancing for pleasure and exhaustion.

Her father had left his entourage of people and stood at the edge of the floor, looking through the crowds. After a moment he caught the flash of Tam's silver dress. The floor was getting thicker with dancers every moment; he didn't elbow his way through but began to dance by himself towards her. Tam, turning, saw him coming, and he whirled up saying: "My dance and my daughter! Sorry, mate!"

He removed Tam from her disappointed partner and, with adroit speed, danced her to the edge of the floor.

They stood panting.

"Go and get your coat and look slippy," he said.

"But Dad! We've only just——"

"No time to argue. Move."

When she ran out of the cloakroom, the Rolls was already drawn up at the door, with her father at the wheel.

"Hop in."

He drove away from the noise and the lights.

Tam was silent, thinking that her father enjoyed making things happen, and whatever it was he was now doing, she wished to God he wouldn't. Some things you just had to leave alone, you couldn't play destiny, you couldn't interfere.

It had begun to rain, the wiper moved slowly to and fro, the water ran in rivulets in front of her eyes. The car drove down suburban roads shining with moisture; it was cold and wet and late and some of the houses were already in darkness. She shifted in her seat and the metallic fringes of her dress made a scraping sound.

"I suppose it's no good asking where you're taking me?"

"None at all."

"A little surprise?"

"That's the ticket."

She felt inclined to sulk, to let him get on with it. She must have been a fool to confide in him and to imagine that he wouldn't try some melodramatic gesture.

It was he who broke the silence.

"Puss. Can you guess where we're going?"

"To see David, I suppose. I don't want to see him. Anyway, I thought he was going to America."

"He's gone."

A wave of sorrow and relief came to her.

"You might call to-night a kind of foray," he said. "Just sit tight and leave it to me."

The great car's engine was so quiet that it scarcely made a sound above the swish of the tyres on the wet surface of the road. She let herself be lulled by the dark and by her father's enigmatic presence. David was gone and love, she supposed, would go too. She had always been told that love went in the end. It would leave her eventually and she would be her "old self," as they said of people who had recovered after an illness. It was hard to believe now that one day she wouldn't be in love any more. But, late or soon, she supposed she would get over him; and meanwhile it was a kind of luxury to let herself be enveloped in her father's strong sway, as real as a heavy cloak.

She looked again through the rain-spattered window of the car; in the distance the sky had begun to glow and some familiar buildings, sparkling with lights, sprang out of the dark. A sign went by.

"Why are we going to the Airport?" she asked, suddenly suspicious.

"I told you, Puss, he has gone. He flew to the States yesterday with my play in his pocket. I want to catch somebody else who may help solve the mystery. We have plenty of time."

He drew up at the "Departures" building, and imperi-

155

ously waving at a man in uniform, informed him that the Rolls must be parked.

"I will let you know when I need it again," he said graciously.

He took Tam's arm and steered her through the late-night travellers to the board of Flight Departures.

"Good, still time," he said, looking up, and ignoring the covert glances from the public, who had already begun to recognise him. "Twenty minutes. Let's have some coffee."

He took her up the moving stairs two at a time, and looked in one or two restaurants before choosing one at the end of a passage.

He pushed open the swing doors and stepped back for Tam to precede him. The restaurant was about to close. Two waiters were stacking chairs and switching off the lamps on the tables. The place had the exaggerated loneliness of a room usually crowded and busy. It was sad. At the far end, alone in a sea of empty tables, and staring through the windows at the airstrip bright with planes, was David.

Tam backed into her father and straight out through the doors again. Safe on the other side of the doors, she said angrily :

"You told me he'd gone! You promised!"

"Oh, stuff!"

She shook him off and would have broken into a run if he hadn't caught her up and pushed her firmly on to a settee. They sat down. Realising that she was now out of David's line of vision, she grew calmer.

"I suppose I ought to be grateful and I suppose it's kind of you to try to help but I don't want to see him again. Ever."

Travellers went by. A disembodied voice spoke of flights to Ankara or Amsterdam, telling travellers that time was short.

"I want to go," Tam said. "He'll come through the door any moment. Please."

"I see you imagine that I drove you all the way here, leaving an excellent party, because I had some corny fancy to do a Friar Lawrence and misguidedly throw Romeo and Juliet together," Robert Waring said. "Tamara, I do not give a fourpenny damn if you don't talk to the boy again. Believe me, you can do as you like. But I do consider that *before* he leaves the country, which he is going to do in ten minutes from now, you should know why he's going. I might add that I think his disappearing act is bloody silly."

She was scarcely listening as she looked nervously at the door.

"I know you mean to be kind——"

"Of course I don't mean to be kind. What clichés you use. When I wish to be kind, I am enormously so. Don't you want to know who that woman *is* in Bryden's life?"

"No."

He smiled.

"I shall tell you. Here's the news. I've been doing some detective work. Bernard has one or two friends in Fleet Street, and with a little digging, the mystery is solved. That female you've been on about is Bryden's mother. Yes. I thought that would stagger you!"

He looked at her with triumph.

"You were so sure he'd married her or been to bed with her. No, Tamara, that is his mother, who is now married to an American with a lot of cash. Bryden's father died years ago."

Tam didn't say a word. She sat with her eyes on him, listening painfully.

"Bernard went to Fleet Street for me. You know those libraries of cuttings the newspapers keep; they're very informative sometimes. The woman off the yacht is called van Eyssen. Forty-five. Quite rich but didn't have a penny when she was married to David's father in the North."

"But why should David leave England because of *her*?"

"His father went to gaol. When David was a lad of thirteen. His dad was a clerk and apparently fixed the books and the poor bastard went to gaol for two years; I expect that woman had expensive tastes. With him in gaol, she left and Bryden was in need of care and protection, as it's called. He went to some kind of orphanage; his father managed to claim him back later."

157

"Oh. Poor David."

"I had a tough childhood myself," said her father unsympathetically. "It's the cold wind that makes the fire flourish. And it's why both David and I understand the human heart. What are you going to do now?"

"Do?" said Tam.

"Gentle heaven, hasn't it occurred to you that he's going into hiding! Into a sort of retreat. It has something to do with sudden success, but it has more to do with you and with me. He's afraid we'll find out this backstreet stuff or that someone will get hold of it and spill the beans. It's quite difficult to find people, you know, if they go away and stew somewhere, using another name; I've known actors who disappeared for years. I don't think he should go, Tamara. He needs us both. Go and tell him that you know all about the murky past and so do I and that we don't give a damn."

"I can't."

"Then I will."

"No!"

He stood up, then, and looked at her.

"I leave you with it, Tamara. I'm going to have a drink. I've told you the story, now you play the next scene without me."

He strode off.

Nobody came out of the restaurant through the swing doors. The ten minutes before David left, that her father had spoken of, went by. She thought of David and the past which can damage the present, and of her father, with his answers to everything. She thought, "If I go running to David and he doesn't want me, I'm asking for love. And wouldn't he feel a kind of pity and perhaps pretend?"

She sat staring at the floor, unable to make up her mind.

A voice exclaimed:

"Tam!"

The doors were swinging to and fro, and there was David, staring as if he couldn't believe his eyes.

"What are you doing here!"

"Dad brought me."

158

The voice echoed over them, chanting that passengers for New York must go to Gate thirty-seven.

"I don't understand—oh God!—that's my plane!"

Tam didn't move.

"Dad knows about it," she said slowly. "About your mother and the trouble your father was in and everything. He said I was to tell you we knew."

"*What did you say!*"

"That my father knows. He told me about it just now. He said to say that it was stupid if you imagined it mattered; it doesn't. I suppose he wants your play. Yes, he does, doesn't he? But I think you want to go. Don't stop because of us, please don't."

She began furiously to rub her eyes.

He bent forward and put his arms round her and closed his eyes and kissed her.

She said, "Goodbye, darling, darling, I do love you but if you want to make a new life——"

"What rubbish are you talking?" he exclaimed. "I'm mad about you. I was going away because things between us were impossible and even work had started to sicken me. My mother was horrible; she thought it a great big laugh that my father had been to prison. She wanted to tell the press at one time—rags to riches, such a lark. I thought you and your father could never——"

They kissed again more violently. The voice floated over them, saying the New York plane was about to leave. They went on kissing as the passengers trooped across the airstrip and climbed into the plane, and minutes later, as they kissed and touched, the plane took off into the dark sky.

At last Tam said :

"I think it's gone."

"I'm sure it has."

"What do we do now?"

"Just stick. Like glue."

"Let's find Dad!"

They set off through the airport, looking into bars and coffee bars. In a corner of the last of these, sitting at the counter and staring at a looking-glass on the wall facing him, was Robert Waring.

Tam, with a bound, put her arms round her father's neck. A waiter, approving, poured two more coffees without being asked.

"He says he wants to stay," said Tam.

"Does he, indeed?"

"For good. With me."

"We'll see."

"Dad!"

"Your father means fine," said David.

Robert Waring looked him up and down.

"Hm. I see you have taken on the role of my interpreter. I'm not sure I need such a person."

"Not even if he writes you exciting plays?"

"Well. There's something in that, of course."

"And what about a part for me?" asked Tam.

"You see," said her father, pointing at her. "You see exactly who you are being unwise enough to take on, my boy."

"I think so."

"Tell me."

"A beautiful girl. A glorious actress. The girl I'm mad about."

"Yes, yes, but the key phrase is missing," said Robert Waring. "It's the last line that counts. She's my daughter, and don't you forget it."